Tor
A Street Boy of Jerusalem

By Florence Morse Kingsley

Author of
Titus, a Comrade of the Cross

Originally Published in 1904

Edited by Phyllis Puetz and Amy Puetz

Golden Prairie Press
P.O. Box 429
Wright, WY 82732

www.AmyPuetz.com

Cover & Layout Design
by Amy Puetz

Printed book ISBN: 978-1-62492-006-6
Ebook ISBN: 978-1-62492-019-6

CONTENTS

Chapter 1
A Stranger Comes to Town

Tor was hungry. Hunger was a common experience in Tor's short life. He merely tightened the dingy rags about his middle and continued to stare at the group of sparrows quarreling noisily in the red dust of the street. It had occurred to Tor that the life of a sparrow must be vastly more pleasant than that of a boy. "They find plenty to eat," he told himself enviously, as he hugged his lean little body. With a sudden impulse the child flung a pebble into the midst of the fowls. The birds shook the dust from their ruffled feathers with noisy clamor of dismay, darted into the bright air, and disappeared far above the tops of the tallest houses.

Tor laughed aloud as a second idea struggled with the first in his clouded brain. Then he checked himself thoughtfully, and winding his rags more closely about him, trotted noiselessly away down the street.

Chelluh, the blind beggar for more years than one could count on the fingers of both hands, and the undisputed proprietor of a snug corner just within the

Damascus gate, was shaking his brazen cup after his daily custom. The cup rattled bravely for certain coins had already been dropped therein by the generous.

"Have mercy, kind lords of Jerusalem. Have mercy on the sorrows of one born blind!" chanted the beggar in his whining monotone. "Kind lords, beautiful ladies, only a denarius, I beseech you, and may the blessings of heaven—" The blind man paused, his quick ear catching the sound of a hesitating foot step amid the hurrying steps which passed in and out at the open gate. "Now may Jove, Jehovah, and all lesser gods be gracious unto thee, noble sir," he began.

Suddenly this professional complainer broke into a bellow of anger and alarm. "Help! Thieves! Murder!" he cried. "My money—my hard-earned money! Someone has stolen my money!" When no one appeared to pay the slightest heed to his outcries, the beggar beat upon the ground in a very fury of impotent rage.

Tor, standing well out of range of the whirling staff, regarded the blind man with a pleased smile. For the moment he had quite forgotten that he was hungry. "Aha! My very good master," he cried tauntingly, "and who is it who will fast today—ay, and perchance tomorrow!"

At sound of the shrill childish voice the beggar sprang to his feet with a vile imprecation. "Is it thou, spawn of the dust, who hast dared to rob me?" he screamed, making a vicious rush in the direction of the voice. "Come hither, that I may break every bone of thy thieving body!"

"What if I choose not to be beaten?" inquired Tor, coolly evading the groping fingers of the beggar. "What if I will to exchange thy good coin for bread? Yesterday thou gave me naught save a beating. Today I have had but a bellyful of curses. I tell thee I will serve thee no longer. May Jove, Jehovah, and all lesser gods be gracious unto thee!"

With this mocking farewell the boy darted away, and being for the moment almost as unseeing as his late master by reason of the hunger which tore him urgently, ran straight into the arms of a man who had been curiously watching the scene from the shelter of an archway.

"Let me go!" shrieked Tor, striving with all his puny strength to writhe out of the powerful grasp of his captor. "Let me go, I say!" Then, like an animal, he twisted about and buried his sharp white teeth in the brown hand that held him.

"Ouf! Verily thou art a wolf-whelp!" cried the stranger, lightly cuffing the child's ears. "Hold hard, small one, till I find how thy matters lie with the fellow yonder."

"Give the lad into the hand of his lawful master, and may heaven reward thee, noble sir," cried Chelluh, making his way rapidly toward the two with the aid of his staff. "The boy is mine—alas, that I should have begotten such an undutiful one. Yet because of mine infirmity—I am helpless, as thou seest—yes, but give him into my hand and I will speedily requite him for robbing me of my last coin."

"Didst thou steal his money, boy?" asked the stranger, stooping to look into the child's pinched face.

"Yes," said Tor, his big, bright eyes fixed upon the beggar in manifest terror. "I was hungry. Let me go or I will bite."

"Ah, little dog, thy teeth shall be broken for that word," mumbled the beggar, feeling after the child with a ferocious chuckle. "Give him to me—ah!"

"Not so fast, friend, not so fast," said the stranger quietly, drawing the boy away from the grimy talons outstretched to seize him. "This is thy son, sayst thou? Why, then, is the child starving and naked, whilst thou art sleek and well covered? Why is he bruised and bleeding like the dog thou didst call him, whilst thou art whole?"

The beggar bared his yellow teeth in a malevolent smile. "Why, herein is a marvel," he said softly. "A noble stranger—for thy speech betrayeth thee, kind sir—come to Jerusalem for the Passover, perchance, for love, for war—the gods alone know thine errand—but delaying his so honorable affairs, his so important business, to look to a blind beggar's brat. Sacred fire, but I am bowed to the earth before thy most noble condescension, who am not worthy to touch the hem of thy honorable garment. I have said that the boy is mine. If he be hungry, if he be naked, if he be bruised—what is that to a stranger from Galilee? Truly, he is but a dog of the gutters, but even a dog hath eyes and may be useful to one in my misfortune."

"Wilt thou that I give thee into the hand of thy father?" asked the Galilean of the child, who no longer struggled to free himself.

"The man is not my father," mumbled Tor hopelessly. "He will kill me."

"You liest, my son, after your custom," put in Chelluh, with a triumphant chuckle. "It is easy to kill—yes, and there is no one to tell me no—easy, but not profitable. I shall discipline you for your profit as is necessary for every son of Abraham. Permit me to salute you, most honorable stranger, 'tis already over long that we keep you from your business—my son and I." And, leaning forward as if to humbly kiss the stranger's robe, the beggar laid violent hands on the trembling child. "Oho! I have my fingers on you at last, rat of the gutter. Come now, and we will settle our matters! Five silver coins it was. Brr—Veil of the temple! What now?"

The stranger had forcibly relaxed the clutch of the bony fingers. "Here is your money," he said, counting out from his broad palm the coins which the child passed over to him with a look of piteous appeal. "Five denarii, said you. As for the lad, if he hath the proper love for you he will doubtless return fast enough when you art in kindlier temper. If not, you art relieved of his keep. Come with me, boy, if you wouldst eat."

"You art a swine!" screamed the beggar. "Dost hear me, Galilean? A swine—swine—swine! Your father, also, and the father of your father, your mother—sacred fire! Help! Help!"

The beggar lay sprawling in the dust, under a well-directed blow from the Galilean's powerful fist. The stranger stood over him, breathing deep, his dark eyes flashing threatening fire. Then, shrugging his shoulders slightly and muttering certain strange words under his breath, he stooped, picked up the beggar quite gently, and set him in his place. "Here is your staff, your cup, and your money, friend," he said calmly, ignoring the torrent of curses which spewed from the open mouth of the beggar like a foul stream. "My Master hath taught me that even such refuse as you must be handled with love. But, hark ye, fellow, no man may defile the name of my mother and stand before Peter, the fisherman."

The beggar strained his sightless eyes after the departing footsteps. "Peter, the fisherman," he repeated with a ferocious smile. "Ah, most honorable and never-to-be-forgotten benefactor, I humbly thank your noble honor for relating to me your name. May, Jove, Jehovah, and all lesser deities enable me to suitably repay the man, and I will offer of my gains a sacrifice—a yearling lamb, no less. I will, I swear it."

Chapter 2
A Sparrow Falleth

The Galilean, having thus made for himself an enemy, plunged into one of the narrow streets leading toward the temple. He was still breathing deep, and thrust his pilgrim's staff fiercely into the red dust of the gloomy thoroughfare. "Who am I that I should follow a prophet?" he demanded of himself angrily. "'If thine enemy smite you, smite not you again,' saith my Master; and behold I have smitten a stranger and one born blind. Verily, I am glad that the Nazarene did not see me do it. Hold, I had forgotten the boy!" He stopped short and presently spied Tor's small head, running over with sunburnt curls, peeping out from the shelter of a projecting archway. The boy's wild, bright eyes met his own defiantly.

"You'll not catch me a second time, Galilean."

The man's white teeth flashed in a quick answering smile. "He who is once bitten by a wolf's whelp in future remembers and is content."

"Did I bite you to bleeding, Galilean?"

"Aye, verily, look you at my hand."

Tor laughed aloud. "It is well," he said briefly.

"Nay, it is not well. 'Tis an evil thing for a child to bite like a dog. Wilt you eat with me, small one?"

"I bite like a dog because I hate like a dog and hunger like a dog," replied Tor slowly. "I stole from the beggar, and you didst take the money from me by force. Which is better? Nay, Galilean, I will not eat with you."

The stranger sat down upon a stone with an air of indifference. "I am hungry," he said, and, producing a brown loaf and a handful of olives from his pouch, began to eat.

Little by little the child crept nearer. Presently he stretched out one puny hand and snatched a fragment of bread which the man carelessly let fall.

"Ah, you?" said the Galilean, with an air of surprise, and let fall another bit. Later he placed a large piece of the bread on the stone at his side and looked away at the tops of the houses.

"Does the hand that bleeds hurt you over much, stranger?" inquired a small voice at his elbow.

"Does a hand that is wounded and bleeding hurt?" repeated the Galilean gravely. "Verily, the smart is grievous; art satisfied?"

"Why didst you hold me when I did not want to be stopped?" inquired the child. "Was my doing any business of thine?"

The man shrugged his shoulders. "Nay," he replied doggedly, "it was not. Moreover, I should have been attending to the beam in mine own eye. I have been taught to forbear quarreling—even for a just cause. I am already punished, and shall be punished again.

'Bray a fool in a mortar,' sayeth the wise Solomon, 'yet will his folly not depart from him.' Such a fool am I."

"Who told you it was an evil thing to fight, Galilean?" asked the boy curiously. He was sitting quite confidently now at the stranger's side, munching bread and olives. "I say it is not evil—that is, unless one is beaten. Then, indeed, it is evil. But one may always curse another. I have learned many strong curses—ay, I am able to curse a man or a beast in many tongues."

"I have a Master, one Jesus of Nazareth," said the Galilean slowly. "He tells me that I must allow a man who has smitten me on one cheek to smite the other also."

"Of course, after you hast smitten thine enemy soundly, he will smite you again, if he is able. Is your Master a gladiator?"

"God forbid!" murmured the Galilean. He stared thoughtfully at the famished child, who was devouring the last crumbs of bread. "Are you filled?" he asked.

Tor shrugged his thin shoulders. "Is the dry bed of Kidron filled with a single shower?" he inquired tersely. "I have eaten. I—" He stopped short and fixed his bright eyes on the Galilean's hurt hand, which he had thrust into a fold of his tunic. "Let me see it," he added timidly.

"Wherefore, wouldst you again whet your teeth on me?"

Tor shook his head. "It hurts me, also, now that I have eaten your bread," he faltered. Then to the immense astonishment of the man, he burst into a passion of weeping, his rough head bowed upon his scarred knees. An evil-looking dog which had been hungrily watching the scene from an angle in the wall skulked rapidly toward the child, and thrust his lean carcass between the two. The Galilean sprang to his feet with a muttered imprecation and threatening upraised staff.

"Stop!" cried Tor, in sudden fury. "It is my dog, Baladan. You shall not strike him!"

The man looked on in horrified amazement while the child wound his thin arms about the shaggy neck of the brute, murmuring gently, "See, here is yet a bit of bread for you, good Baladan. Eat, my friend, eat, it is good bread."

The dog licked the child's bare feet and whined his delight. "Do you not know, boy, that dogs are unclean and evil brutes?" demanded the Galilean with an air of profound disgust. "Nay, you art thyself unclean and evil yourself, and, I must go away to my Master." He turned his back upon the child and strode away, his head bent, his eyes fixed gloomily upon the ground.

Tor watched him furtively. Then, with a word to the dog, which obediently slunk back into his chosen lair, he trotted noiselessly after the man. "I will see where the stranger goes," he told himself.

The child had not followed the Galilean far when the dull rumbling of chariot-wheels and the sharp crack of a whip warned him out of the narrow thoroughfare. He flattened himself against a convenient wall and stared greedily at the sight. This could be no less than a Roman official of high rank; the boy knew it right well. His eyes roved eagerly over the rich ornaments of the chariot, and fastened inquiringly on the frowning face of the man who guided the plunging horses. A second man stood at the driver's side, a man wearing a tunic and toga richly bordered with the imperial purple.

Tor drew his breath sharply in pleased astonishment. Then he saw that the chariot was hotly pursued by a crowd of gamins like himself.

"'Tis the Roman Pilate himself," he chuckled, "and perchance he will presently cast out coins like grain from the fat pouch at his belt."

A shrill cry burst from the child's lips as he joined the rabble at the chariot-wheels. To run, to shout, to feel the glad thud of the falling coin; to wrestle fiercely in the dust, to arise victorious, to eat and drink the fruits of conquest—this was no new thing to Tor. And what, indeed, was the random sting of a Roman lash—even when it chanced to fall on naked limbs or shoulders—to the glory of the chase?

The man who held the whip plied it vigorously before and behind with loud imprecations in an unknown tongue, while he who wore the imperial purple stared frowningly into vacancy, his hands clasped loosely behind his back.

Tor's swift feet gained on the chariot. "Hail, great Pilate!" he shouted impudently, "Art deaf? Art blind? Art paralyzed? Give us now of the temple treasure! Ay—give! Give!"

The Roman's dull eyes flashed baleful fire. The fact that he had attempted to seize large sums from the temple treasuries, and that the Jews hated him for it, was no secret in Jerusalem. But must the very street urchins taunt him with the fact? He snatched the lash from the driver and plied it himself with a practiced hand.

Tor fell back with a shriek of keenest agony.

The chariot and the rabble swept on and disappeared, leaving the child writhing on the pavement like a wounded animal.

The whip, fringed cruelly with glistening barbs of steel, had lashed him full across the eyes.

Chapter 3
The Man Who Opened His Eyes

To Tor, groaning in the wordless anguish of his hurts, came a soft inquiring touch on his heaving shoulders. Led by that kind instinct which guides all wounded creatures, the child had crawled away and hidden himself from unfriendly eyes in the mouth of a ruinous sewer near by. Here he had lain long hours, exhausted with agony. The dog snuffed the small huddled figure from head to foot with short, anxious whines. Then he fell to industriously licking the one limp brown hand which crept out from beneath the ragged tunic.

"Baladan," whispered Tor, and shrieked aloud with the intolerable smart of rising tears in his blinded eyes.

The shriek, faint as it was, reached the ears of a second boy, who was searching carefully from side to side of the gloomy little thoroughfare. "Is that you, Tor," he exclaimed, stooping to stare in at the sewer's mouth. "Are you badly hurt?"

"Oh, Dan, the accursed lash of the Roman smote my eyes," groaned the child, and sputtered out some strange curse in the Egyptian tongue, which he had learned from his late master.

The second boy pursed up his coarse lips into a soft whistle of comprehension. Then he bent down and stared briefly into the drooped face of the half-delirious sufferer. "One more blind beggar in Jerusalem." he murmured, smiting his bare thigh with closed fist. Then raising his fingers to his lips he gave vent to a shrill cry of summons. It was promptly answered by the soft thud of a water-carrier's feet and the loud tinkle of his brazen cups.

"Give him to drink," commanded Dan, indicating Tor with a grimy forefinger. "The poor fool hath brought ill-fortune upon himself. 'Tis the evil eye of a surety." With that he produced a copper coin, which the water-carrier acknowledged with a cup of water from the goat-skin on his back.

"I will come again at sunset and give him a drink," said the water-carrier, with a sidelong glance of fear and pity. Then the two departed, leaving Tor to his misery.

How the child lived through the days and weeks that followed only Baladan knew. The dog warmed his master's pinched body at night, keeping at bay other prowling beasts of the outcast race which ranged the deserted streets, as lawless and almost as fierce as wolves.

He even fed him, more than once bringing fragments of bread and fish, stolen from a vender's stall at the imminent peril of his life. Occasionally the friendly water-carrier visited the suffering boy, and the little wild children of the street, swarming like sparrows in the streets of Jerusalem, shared their infrequent crusts with him.

By slow degrees the anguish of his wounds grew less poignant. The cruelly disfigured eyes were indeed wholly darkened, but they ceased to send burning shafts of fire to the tortured brain. The child slept fitfully, ate what he could get, and one day even smiled when Baladan brought him a meatless bone, laying it down at his feet with extravagant expressions of satisfaction. "Nay, good Baladan," murmured Tor, patting his friend's shaggy coat, "Indeed I am not hungry today. Eat, dear beast," and he thrust the bone into the dog's mouth, and closed his sharp teeth upon it. Baladan understood, and the two rested together in the sunshine with the appearance of real contentment.

The charitable water-carrier had bestowed one of his brass-like cups upon the blind boy, and this with his ruined eyes became his stock in trade. Little by little he learned to send forth the sorrowful cry of the blind beggar. After a time he could find his way from place to place with the aid of the dog. And so it came to pass that there was one more blind beggar in Jerusalem.

Once during these evil days of his darkness, Tor fell in with his old master. This is how it happened: the child, having grown bolder, had made his way farther than his previous habit. He moved into the more crowded thoroughfares of the city, and there his shrill cry for alms sounded loud and clear above the tumult of the marketplace. He rattled his cup bravely as was the custom of the professional beggar, sending forth into the unfriendly world the old familiar cry of the beggar, Chelluh. "Have mercy, kind lords of Jerusalem, have mercy on the sorrows of one born blind! Kind lord, kind lady, only a denarius, I beseech you, and may Jehovah and all lesser gods be gracious unto you!"

Now it chanced that Chelluh himself had also come to the marketplace to beg alms, and, hearing the child's voice afar off, recognized it with the unerring ear of the blind. "Fetch me now to the voice that crieth my cry," he commanded the one that led him. And when presently he was come to the place where Tor stood in the safe angle of two windowless walls, he stopped short with an evil smile.

"Are you of a surety blind, my son—that you stealest my cry for alms as you didst once steal my money?" he demanded.

Tor trembled like a leaf in the wind at sound of the cruel voice. "Alas, I am indeed blind, good master," he said beseechingly. "Have mercy upon me, for I—"

The prayer ended in a muffled shriek for help as the blind man hurled himself upon the blind child, griping him in a very fury of malicious hatred. No one interfered. What, indeed, was the quarrel of two beggars in an angle of the wall?

Trade pressed hard in Jerusalem as elsewhere, and a man must mind naught save his own business if he would prosper. So no one glanced that way when the blind man, having satisfied his lust for revenge, departed, leaving the child's limp body upon the ground.

Tor was not dead. He was only bruised and beaten and choked into insensibility, and after awhile he revived and crawled feebly away with the faithful Baladan, His begging-cup was gone, and he no longer dared to raise his voice to crave alms from the passersby. Occasionally one tossed him a coin or a crust, but for the most part the child crouched all day in his corner motionless, starving. The days and weeks dragged by.

He was sitting thus one morning when the sun had climbed high enough to flood his darkened nook with yellow light. Tor could feel the warmth of its radiance in his chill darkness. He sighed deeply and spread forth his lean hands, wondering dully what it would be like to see once more. He had already forgotten the blue sky and the moving clouds, the flutter of green leaves over high garden walls and the glistening whir of bird-wings in the sunshine. His night was endless, unbroken by morning gleam or noontide glory. It meant cold and hunger and a thousand nameless miseries which he endured because he must endure. It would stretch on and on, he thought, to some far-off, hopeless end, when perchance he might sleep to awaken no more.

Tor had looked upon such sleepers with a scared creeping of the flesh in the old days of seeing. Now the sleep seemed good, and quite stupidly and vaguely he longed for it.

Somewhere, afar off, there was shouting and a sound of voices that chanted musically. The child listened with the sharpened attention which had grown to be his one defense and solace. In the old days his flying feet would have borne him swiftly enough to see what was happening. Now he could only listen, and wonder.

"Perhaps 'tis some great prince come to Jerusalem," he muttered, and tried to picture to himself the bright pageant of the marching troops, the gorgeous uniforms, the jeweled robes of the nobles, the chariots, the horses. And now the shouting grew louder, there was a noise of swift-hurrying feet, of confused questions and answers, while above all rose the clear musical voices of myriads of children crying in the rhythmic measures of the temple chorals, "Hosanna to the Son of David! Blessed— Blessed is the King that comes in the name of the Lord! Hosanna in the highest!"

Tor started uncertainly to his feet, a strange, new longing for something he knew not what stealing into his starved soul. Baladan whined uneasily, then, running to the street corner and back again to his helpless master, began to utter short excited barks.

The child's thin fingers trailed the rough wall. His timid feet crept nearer to the jubilant procession. "Hosanna! Hosanna to the King! Hosanna to the Son of David!" He had reached the open square, and, fearing to go further, he sank down once more in the shelter of a friendly column, hot tears stealing from his darkened eyes. "Oh, Baladan," he moaned, "If I could only see!"

And now the sweet chanting was growing gradually fainter. Tor followed the procession in fancy. It was moving toward the temple, he knew, that great pile of stone and marble and gold which towered above the tumultuous streets of Jerusalem like the glistening palace of a dream. Now it had passed into the outer courts, and a great and singular silence fell upon the city.

It was broken after what seemed hours of waiting by light and rapid footfalls. "Tor," cried an eager, breathless voice. "Where are you? Tor!"

"Here!" answered the blind boy, starting to his feet and straining his sightless eyes in the direction of the voice. "Here am I. What do you want, Dan?" For he knew the voice and the step of his friend.

"I have come to fetch you to the temple," breathed the boy excitedly. "You must come quickly, before the King has gone away to his palace."

"Did the King scatter coins among the crowd?" asked Tor eagerly. "Are the soldiers giving bread and alms to the people, as when Pilate came to Jerusalem?"

"Nay, the man is like no other great one who ever came to Jerusalem," answered Dan wonderingly. "He is truly a King though. Did you not hear the people shouting, 'Blessed is the King that cometh!' Hark you, the man is a strange King. He wears no crown, no jewels; he hath no soldiers, no money for the people. He came into the city riding on the colt of a donkey; but the people cast even their garments upon the earth before him. I saw it, and shouted with the rest; and because I had no coat, I cut a green branch from a tree and cast it beneath the feet of his beast. So also did many others, when they saw what I had done. They cut palm-branches, olive-branches, and acacias from fields and gardens all along the way; 'twas a great sight! The big turbans came out in a rage to shut our mouths, but for once they could not. Come, you must come!"

"Why should I come?" said Tor mournfully. "I am only a beggar—and blind."

"But you shalt have thine eyes again, lad," cried Dan exultantly. "The King is even now laying his hands upon the blind, the lame, and paralyzed, and they see and leap and walk forthwith. I myself have looked upon it. I will fetch you to him."

"But the King would not touch me—a beggar, and unclean," wailed Tor. "Look you, I am no better than Baladan, and the Jews hate and despise all dogs. He would spurn me—spit upon me. Nay, I will not go."

Dan laid violent hands upon the blind boy. "You shalt go with me," he said loudly. "I have said it. I will take you to the King, then if he rejects you—spits upon you—nay, but he will not reject you; I saw him, and I say that he will not. But if he heal you not, what then? I will bring you again to this place. There shall no harm befall you."

The two boys made their way to the temple enclosure, slipping easily among the excited multitudes, unnoticed even as the little brown sparrows which flit among the great feet of horses in a crowded thoroughfare. And when they had come to the place where Jesus was, they found already gathered great numbers of blind and lame and withered and paralyzed, and the court ringing with the noise of their petitions mingled with the jubilant thanksgivings of those already healed.

"Here, get you betwixt these two cripples," whispered Dan urgently. "Fasten onto this man's tunic—so! Now go, and come again—seeing. I will wait for you by this third pillar. You wilt see me."

The blind boy stumbled on behind his crippled guide, his heart beating so loud in his ears that he could scarce hear what the Voice said to him. But the thrilling touch on his sightless eyes sank to the depths of his soul. He saw—Jesus.

Someone was pushing him from behind. Tor yielded to the pressure without a word—without a sound. His great eyes, wide and bright, still remained fastened upon the man who had healed him, but he uttered no sound of rejoicing.

To Dan, watching beside the third pillar, came a sudden sickening sense of defeat. He made his way through the crowd and again laid forcible hands upon Tor.

"Let me alone," commanded Tor briefly. "I want to look at the man."

"Can you see him?" inquired Dan incredulously.

Tor made no answer. He was thinking confusedly, vaguely, while one fixed purpose formed and lifted itself like a great, radiant light in his darkened understanding. "I shall follow him," he said aloud, and his thin face shone strangely. "I shall see him always."

"Can you see, lad?" cried Dan, griping his friend's shoulders impatiently, "or are you crazed as well as blind?"

Tor turned his bright eyes upon the other boy. "Can I see?" he echoed, and laughed aloud. Then, in a sudden ecstasy, he leaped upon a balustrade and shouted aloud the word which he had heard afar off in his darkness, "Hosanna! Hosanna! Hosanna in the highest!" Myriads of children's voices took up the cry, and it arose into the blue heavens far—far beyond the smoke of the sacrificial fires, till it mingled with the songs of angels before the great white throne. And there was joy in Heaven.

Chapter 4
The King, My Master!

The sun was setting behind the mountains before hunger, more potent than even the temple police with its flail-like rods of office, had cleared the great court of the temple. The sick and blind, the maimed and paralyzed had gone away restored, the multitude, in awe of the miracles and weary of shouting, followed. The Nazarene himself, looking more worn and thoughtful than his wont, also departed with the twelve, his disciples bearing themselves haughtily under the angry eyes of the priests.

At last their Master had declared himself before the nation. All the city had heard the royal acclamation. The promised reign of the house of David was about to be restored in Jerusalem. Already they felt themselves to be princes and governors in a kingdom of unimagined splendor.

Peter, the Galilean, as he followed with the others after the pale, potent worker of miracles, who was also a King, became aware of a determined clutch upon his robe, and, looking down, beheld with amazement and displeasure the small, pinched face of Tor. "I have nothing for you, beggar," he said quickly, and pulled his garment impatiently away from the child's clinging touch.

"Nay, but I am not begging," said Tor, in nowise abashed. "The man—yonder—is he your Master?"

"What is that to you?" frowned the future prince of Israel. "Get you gone, the King is passing."

"The King—your Master—healed me just now of blindness," persisted the child. "What is his name? Nay, I will not let loose of you until I know."

"His name is Jesus," said Peter unwillingly. "Now begone."

"I will not," said Tor positively, "for I also have chosen him for my Master." But he loosed his hold on the man's garment and fell back a few paces. "I shall follow him," he told himself simply.

Just what he expected from his new Master Tor could have told no one. He did not put the question to himself. He was again both hungry and thirsty, but he had cared little for either hunger or thirst in his evil past. Now he tightened the rags cheerfully about his middle in the old familiar way and trotted noiselessly after the little group of men, in the midst of which walked his Master.

The child was trying dully to recall what the Galilean had said concerning this man on the day he had delivered him out of the hand of Chelluh by the Damascus gate.

The thought of Chelluh brought a new purpose uppermost in his thoughts. "When I find a convenient season from following my Master I will return and beat the blind beggar even as he beat me," he promised himself, with a new and savage joy in his restored sight. "He that hath eyes is truly a god, and to know this one might well be blind for a season."

His new Master, surrounded by his little guard, had passed out of the city by this time, and all were walking swiftly on one of the level Roman roads which bound Jerusalem to its heathen Emperor. Tor followed unperceived in the gathering dusk of evening. After a little while the party reached a small village, entered it, and paused before a large and beautiful garden enclosure, where they were evidently expected, for they were immediately admitted and the doors shut solidly behind them.

Tor marked the place well, then, not knowing what else to do, he returned to Jerusalem, found Baladan, and spent the night in one of his old haunts near the Damascus Gate.

When the child awoke in the morning, the marvelous events of the previous day floated before his wide eyes like the misty fragments of a half-forgotten dream. "Was I indeed blind?" he asked himself. "Or was that also an evil dream of night?" Baladan's anxious whine recalled him more fully to his waking senses, and he sprang up to find Dan throwing olive-stones at him from a neighboring wall. "Sleepy-head!" laughed the beggar, discharging another volley of stones. "Look you, lad, there is much to be seen in Jerusalem today—if, indeed, the man restored your sight. The Passover pilgrims are coming in by thousands. I have already begged breakfast for me and for you."

"I can see as well as ever," said Tor briefly. "But I must first find my Master. Give me the loaf and I will go."

"Beggar!" cried Dan, tossing his comrade a fragment of a loaf and half a dozen olives, "what hast you to do with a King? Come, we will lead a merry life this week. The pilgrims are laden with goods, and one with light fingers and lighter heels need lack nothing." The boy snapped his brown fingers and executed a sort of savage dance in the exuberance of his spirits.

"He said, 'Do not beat thine enemy; but if thine enemy smite you, let him smite you again, if he will,'" said Tor, munching his bread reflectively. "There is Chelluh, he hath beaten me, not once nor twice only, but many times."

"Who said 'Do not smite thine enemy?'" demanded Dan, staring.

"My Master said it. He said it to the Galilean, not to me. I will, therefore, beat Chelluh, I will also steal his money and give it to my Master."

"My Master—my Master!" mocked Dan. "How dost you know that the man will have you for a servant?"

"I do not know, but if I will serve him, then will he be my Master whether he will or not. And I will serve him. I have said it."

"How?" persisted Dan.

Tor stared about him reflectively. "I will bring him blind folks to heal," he said at last. "I can do that."

"You are a rare fool," said Dan conclusively. "I am going to the pilgrim encampment outside the walls.

Look you beggar, when you are through serving the King, your Master, you wilt find me there eating the fat and drinking the sweet," and with a laugh of scorn the boy darted away.

Left to himself, Tor sat for a long time deep in thought. An astonishing picture had presented itself to his mind. The child seemed to see himself leading his old master, Chelluh, to the healing King, and Chelluh, restored to sight, crying, "Hosanna, hosanna in the highest!"

Far off and faint upon the morning air a voice arose, rising and falling in a sad monotone. Tor knew it. It was the voice of Chelluh begging alms.

He arose and ran with swift feet to the place which he had hated and avoided even in his dreams, and there in the familiar angle of the wall sat the beggar, shaking his empty cup, the sun falling full upon his evil face. Tor stood quite still and gazed at the blind man with his Christ-touched eyes, and for the first time in his short life, loving pity for another welled up within him. "Master," he said, in a low voice. Then he drew nearer, and spoke in a louder voice, "Chelluh." He would call no man master save one.

The blind beggar beat upon his cup with his bony knuckles. "Who calls me?" he asked, scarce believing his truthful ears which told him whose voice had spoken. "Who calls me?" he repeated, trembling. "I choked the little dog to death, yet it is his voice that speaks."

"You didst not kill me," said Tor. "I am alive, and see once more. Yesterday the King, my Master, healed me."

"Lies!" mumbled Chelluh, shaking his great head, "you wast always a liar."

"This is no lie that I tell you. Wouldst you receive your sight also? Come, I will lead you to my Master. He will heal you."

Chelluh reflected for a moment. Physically he was stronger than the puny child. Yet he distrusted his words. "You are plotting mischief against me, gutter rat," he growled, "I know you."

"If I plotted mischief I should have come upon you suddenly, and run away before you were aware of me," replied Tor. "I am no man's fool, but I serve a new Master, one Jesus. 'Tis for my Master I do this. He heals blind folk, therefore I fetch blind folk to him to be healed. Thus I serve my Master. Wilt you come?"

Chelluh rose slowly to his feet. "I will come," he said, "but if you hast lied to me, little dog, you knowest the strength of my hands, and shalt know it again. This time I will perhaps kill you.

Tor shuddered at the familiar clutch of the knotted fingers on his slender shoulders. Yet he walked bravely forward. "So I serve my Master," he said aloud.

Chapter 5

Deep Calleth Unto Deep

"Where is the man who heals the blind?" demanded Chelluh, leaning heavily on the child.

Tor trembled, but he answered boldly enough. "He will be in the court of the Gentiles healing the blind."

There was a great concourse of people crowding the street which led up to the temple, and amongst them numerous cripples, paralyzed men on litters, sick children in the arms of anxious, wild-eyed mothers, and blind beggars, led like Chelluh by willing guides.

"Yes, the King is in the temple," repeated Tor confidently. Then he shouted, "hosanna" in his shrill childish voice, as he had done the day before. The cry was echoed by myriads of voices both far and near.

Chelluh's heavy hand descended upon his guides curly head. "Be silent, fool," he hissed. "There is tumult ahead. Keep clear of the crowd, I say, and look sharp!"

They were near the main entrance of the temple now, and the stream of newcomers was met by an excited mob of people coming out. Imprecations, shouts, and loud angry cries blended confusedly with the whir of moving wings, for a great cloud of doves hovered uncertainly over the place, now flying, now settling on the roofs and pinnacles of the marble porticoes. Chelluh stopped determinedly and snuffed the air like an animal. "What is going on within?" he demanded of Tor.

The question was answered by a woman in a foreign headdress who chanced to pause in the crowd beside them. "The Nazarene has thrust out the sellers of doves and the moneychangers from the great court," she said laughingly. "With these eyes I saw it. The Prophet cast down the tables with no gentle hand, loosed the doves, and drove out the craven Jews before him like a flock of frightened sheep. 'Twas a great sight. Also, the money was scattered all over the court among the multitude. Even I, a Gentile, am the richer for it."

"Money?" exclaimed the blind beggar greedily. "Come, let us go in, I would I had eyes that I might glean of this harvest."

"The man gives eyes also for the asking," said the woman indifferently. "I have witnessed miracles of healing till I am weary of them. The Jew is a great magician, surely, but his own countrymen hate him, and the Romans care naught for miracles, so betwixt the two he will perchance fall to the ground."

Tor was not listening, he was watching for a good opening through which to pilot his blind charge.

"When you are healed, you wilt become a servant of the King," he said softly in the ear of the blind beggar.

"Ay, and will I?" sneered Chelluh, "and what will I do then?"

"Fetch blind folks to be healed," said the child simply. "Now I see him," he added, with joyful certainty. "Follow quickly and you shalt be blind no longer!"

Like the showers and sunshine of the Father which bless the good and the evil alike through all the years of all the ages, so was the healing power of him who manifested the Father in every act of his life. And so it came to pass that many came to be healed of blindness in those last great days, and went away with seeing eyes and blind souls.

Chelluh's first act after receiving his sight was to stare hard at Tor. The boy shivered beneath his gaze. Chelluh with seeing eyes was even more terrible than Chelluh blind. Those devouring eyes were roving like the eyes of a beast of prey over the excited crowd. They fastened at last on a man who stood not far from the Nazarene. "I know that man's voice," said Chelluh. "Who and what is he?"

"He is a servant of the King," said Tor. "His name is Peter."

"His name is Peter," repeated Chelluh, and struck his palms together softly. He turned and without another word plunged into the crowd and was gone.

Tor forgot him presently. He was edging his way nearer and nearer to the wondrous Voice. Jesus was teaching the people, and his words fell upon the child's ignorant ears with a strange and potent charm. He could not understand, but he listened because he loved, and listening and loving, he comprehended something of what was being said, even as a babe discerns the speech of its mother. Love answereth love, as deep calleth unto deep.

At night Tor followed his Master and the twelve when they went out of the city to lodge in the house of his friends in Bethany. This time the child slept on the ground in the shelter of the garden wall, begging a crust and a cup of water from one of the villagers at dawn. No one questioned the boy and so he was able again to follow almost at their heels when the little party set out for Jerusalem.

There was a withered fig tree near the wayside, and Tor heard the Galilean, Peter, pause and say to his Master, "Rabbi, behold the fig tree which you cursed is withered away."

And Jesus looked upon the withered tree and answered the Galilean on this wise, "Have faith in God; for I tell you that whosoever shall say unto this mountain, Be you taken up and cast into the sea, and shall not doubt in his heart, but shall believe that what he saith cometh to pass; he shall have it. Therefore I say unto you, All things whatsoever ye pray and ask for, *believe that ye have received them*, and ye shall have them. And whensoever ye stand praying, forgive, if ye have aught against any one; that your Father also which is in heaven may forgive you your trespasses."

Tor was crouching in the shelter of a bush and heard every word distinctly. His thin face burned with excitement. "He said 'whosoever,' "he murmured. "He said 'whosoever.' "Tor knew something of the custom of prayer. Many times he had seen the rich Pharisees standing motionless at the street-corners praying. Also, he had begged in the temple court, where many persons prayed aloud. For himself, he never prayed. The God of the Jews regarded not beggars, he told himself. Now as he crouched behind the bush, listening to the departing footsteps of the thirteen men, he began to say over to himself the word "Father," which the man who had opened his eyes said so often.

He repeated it softly to himself many times. Then he sprang up and followed hard after his Master, vaguely comforted and glad at heart.

The day was a long one, passed mainly in the great Court of the Gentiles, and Tor, mingling with every gaping crowd which surrounded the Nazarene, was puzzled and troubled by much that he saw and heard. There was no shouting of "hosanna" today, no royal acclamations. The people stood close together and listened doubtfully to the strange teachings of the King in the seamless robe—the King who wore no crown and whose followers bore no arms. He was telling stories to the multitude, stories so simple that even a beggar could understand them. The child pressed close, so close that he could have touched the sandaled feet of the man who had opened his eyes. And so he listened to the stories of the father and his two undutiful sons, the absent lord of the vineyard and his wicked servants, the generous king who made a marriage feast for his son, and how it befell that the very beggars were gathered into the feast. The child smiled and trembled and wept aloud beneath the power of that wondrous Voice. More than once the Master's deep eyes rested upon the small upturned face with its wistful look of adoration.

And once, as he was speaking, the hand of Jesus rested for a moment on the rough curls of the beggar's head. Ah, the rapture of that moment! Tor knew now deep in his heart that he was the accepted servant of the King. He could have remained there forever listening to the stories, but the temple police began to clear away the crowd with loud authoritative cries and random thrusts of their gold cover poles of office.

"Make way!" they shouted. "Make way for the holy and reverend chief priests and the honorable elders of the Sanhedrin!"

Through the narrow passage thus cleared there came presently in great pomp and glory a stately delegation from the supreme council of the Jewish rulers. The chief priests wished to question publicly this worker of miracles—this teller of strange parables, who openly performed his mighty works in the temple of Jehovah without their will or permission. "By what authority doest you these things?" they demanded. "And who gave you this authority?"

Jesus, calm and unafraid, answered them after their own custom with another question. "I also will ask you one thing," he said, "which if you tell me, I likewise will tell you by what authority I do these things. The baptism of John, whence was it? From heaven or from men?"

The gorgeously-robed official who had asked the question glanced about him at the hostile faces of the multitude, with a defiant air of scorn and contempt. Mumbling and stammering angrily, he turned and conferred in a whisper with his companions. "If we say, "From heaven," he muttered, "the fellow will ask, Why then did you not believe him?"

"True," spoke another, "but if we say, from men, there is the multitude to be reckoned with, for they all hold that John was a prophet."

And so they presently faced the Master, their fierce eyes under the glittering insignia of the priestly office glaring at the calm, pale Man of Nazareth. "We know not," they said.

And Jesus replied, "Neither will I tell you by what authority I do these things."

The priests withdrew in sullen silence, and the telling of strange stories went on, but Tor, somehow swept from his position by the shifting crowd, found himself near the defeated priests. They had paused to listen with the others, and were standing with folded arms and sneering faces by one of the great pillars of the portico.

Tor slipped behind the column, suddenly to listen to them. These men were speaking in a half whisper of the King, his Master. They hated him. Tor was sure of it! "The fellow will ruin us if we cannot stop his blatant mouth," said one. "Listen now to his open threats, 'The kingdom of God shall be taken away from you, and shall be given to a nation bringing forth the fruits thereof.'"

"And he calls himself our King," sneered another. "A pretty pass hath the chosen people come to when the rabble choose a Nazareth carpenter for King. Aha, I laugh at him!"

"'Tis no time for mirth," growled another. "The multitudes are always interested in some new thing. Stoning or crucifixion is better than laughter for such a one. Hark you, the thing must be put down and speedily. I know a way and a man. He—" The voice dropped to low whispers, and Tor, trembling with vague fright, and scarce knowing what he did, wriggled his way through the crowd toward the white-robed figure of Jesus.

Peter, the Galilean, was also talking excitedly with a man in the outskirts of the crowd. Tor fixed his eyes upon the tall, broad-shouldered fisherman with some confidence. "I will tell him," he said to himself, and hovered expectantly near, waiting for an opportunity to speak. "He must declare himself unmistakably and at once," the small, dark-faced man was saying with an impatient gesture. "This telling of pretty tales and working of miracles has gone on too long. We should arm ourselves and make ready, and the Sanhedrin must be won over by some great sign from heaven. We can do nothing without them."

"And I say let the Master work out his plans as it pleases him," said Peter boldly. "Did you not see his kingly air on Sunday, Judas? He is every inch a King, I tell you, and able to make of us princes and high priests—yes, and to sweep away all oppressors by the word of his mouth."

"Able, perhaps," muttered Judas shaking his head, "but I doubt him. The man cares nothing for money—nothing for power. I know him. What are his plans? Does anyone know them? Do we who are nearest him dare ask him? He is, perchance, nothing more than a dreamer, and our ambitions and hopes are founded upon the shifting sands of his visions. Nay, I know what you wouldst say, Simon. But you are no statesman—no patriot. I hear the chosen people groaning in their slavery. I see the iron heel of Rome about to crush out the last lingering life of the nation. Will this man save us? Can he, I ask? Or is he—" Judas choked convulsively, and tore at the neck of his garment with quivering hands. "I am half mad with the torture of it," he groaned, "the—the waiting—the doubt. I—I fear that he—"

"Nay, you a rebel and unbelieving fellow at heart," said Peter easily. "Didst hear how the Master answered the priests just now? I could have laughed aloud to see them slink away like whipped dogs."

"Like whipped dogs—yes," muttered the other. "But they will return another time like ravening wolves, unless he declares himself. 'Tis folly— folly!" He turned and plunged hastily into the crowd, and Peter, left to himself, began to smite his great hands softly together. "He hath the power to put them all to silence," he said half aloud. "He will do it—let no one fear!"

"I fear," said Tor, suddenly speaking at the fisherman's elbow. "*I fear—for him.*"

"What now, small one," muttered Peter, staring down at the child with a displeased shrug. "Have I not told you to keep your distance?"

"Yes, but I will not," said Tor doggedly. "Listen, Galilean. I heard the men in long robes speak of him. They hate him. They will kill him, if they can. Take care of him!"

"My Master can take care of himself, boy," said Peter boastfully. "He is a King, also, I am his servant."

"Where is your sword, servant of a King!" demanded Tor, eying him doubtfully.

"My sword—my sword?" stammered the fisherman. "I have no sword."

"Then get one," advised Tor briefly.

Chapter 6
Rejected of Men

The Galilean shook his great shoulders doubtfully as he stared after the small, agile figure of the boy, darting and doubling, twisting and turning through the huddled masses of people gathered about his Master. "By the double veil—" he began, and stopped short with a perplexed frown. "'Swear not at all,' saith my Master, yet my unruly tongue constantly betrays me. Truly, the tongue is a fire, tamed by no man, not even its owner."

There was some new excitement brewing, for the fisherman was thrust rudely to one side by a guard of brawny temple police, who advanced as before, crying out to the people to fall back in the name of the Sanhedrin. The group of men which followed close on the heels of the guard forced another profane exclamation from the unguarded lips of the Galilean. "Herodians!" he muttered, "and Pharisees. Now, what doth this mean?"

The question was answered by Judas, who reappeared at that moment, his dark face distorted by a savage sneer. "Wouldst know why these courtiers of Herod have come to the Nazarene, Fisherman? Well, I can tell you. Our chosen Master hath of late permitted himself to be hailed King of the Jews, yet hath he not pledged the nation to the support of his claim, nor even armed us, his chosen followers. What then? Herod is a despicable tetrarch of Galilee. You mayst know, Fisherman—unless your head is too thick for understanding—that the claims of the carpenter's son have been widely noised abroad, and have already reached the ears of royal Herod. Jesus of Nazareth must take heed or he will presently be dealt with after the manner of John the Baptist—or worse."

"Get you behind me, prophet of evil," growled Peter, "you hast ever the dismal croak of the raven. What if Herod intends to acknowledge Jesus as the lawful descendant of David and the promised Messiah?"

Judas laughed silently, his narrow eye-slits shooting arrows of scorn at the big fisherman. "What if the stones of the temple should suddenly become armed troops for the defense of our wise Master?" he asked.

"It might well be so," murmured Peter thoughtfully. "Did he not walk upon the sea? Did he not control the lightning and the tempest? Did he not feed the five thousand with one man's meal? Listen now, they are speaking to him!"

The court officials of Herod, dressed in rich robes, perfumed and smiling, were addressing themselves to the man of Nazareth. They prefaced their words with extravagant bows of mockery. Behind them stood the Pharisees, alert and watchful.

"Listen!" repeated the fisherman, his honest face flushed with expectancy.

"We know that you are true, Rabbi," began the spokesman of the party, "and carest for the opinion of no man; for you regardest not the person of men, but teachest the way of God in truth. Is it lawful to give tribute unto Caesar, or not? Shall we give, or shall we not give?"

Jesus faced his inquisitors, erect and calm, his deep eyes searching their hypocritical hearts. There was silence for a full minute, while the crowded listeners craned their necks for his reply, and Judas clenched his knotted hands in a very agony of suspense. This was the supreme moment. Tribute to Caesar, or not? Tribute to the usurping heathen emperor, or allegiance to the throne of David—which?

The carpenter's son whitened slowly under the fiery eyes which scorched him with their brutal passions. Then came his answer—spoken slowly, deliberately, "Why tempt ye me? Give me a penny, that I may see it."

The official from Herod's court languidly fingered the gold pieces in his pouch, with a pitying smile for this penniless pretender to a throne, and presently, drawing out one of the lesser coins of the empire, gave it to the Nazarene.

"Whose is this image and superscription?" demanded Jesus, his voice ringing out in the crowded place like the peal of a great bell.

"Caesar's," replied the officer, bowing as a servant at the mention of that name of power.

Then came the wondrous answer, forever solving all questions of human allegiance, "Render unto Caesar the things that are Caesar's, and unto God the things that are God's."

Instantly there arose from the multitude a great hum of approval. "Well spoken!" "We have a Solomon in our midst!" burst from one and another in deep-throated chorus. And the Pharisees, angry and threatening, withdrew with the downcast Herodians.

"Did I not say that he was a match for the best of them?" cried Peter, showing his white teeth in a great laugh of relief and triumph. "Yes, our Master is a king surely, wiser than any scribe, keener than a Damascus blade having two edges."

But Judas groaned aloud. "What a moment to have declared himself!" he muttered. "He lost his opportunity. What and who is the man?"

Tor had wriggled his small body through the dense crowd back to the feet of Jesus, where he crouched ready to spring like a faithful dog at the throat of any man who should threaten his Master. "I have no sword," muttered the child to himself, "but I have two hands well furnished with nails, also, I have teeth like the teeth of Baladan. Let the men in long robes beware."

But as yet no man dared to lay so much as a finger on that seamless robe. Other tempters wearing great turbans, bearded, scowling, came to ask mocking questions concerning the resurrection. And on the heartless men of the multitude fell those significant words which the world has neither comprehended nor believed to this day, "But as touching the resurrection of the dead, have you not read that which was spoken unto you by God, saying, I am the God of Abraham, and the God of Isaac, and the God of Jacob? *God is not the God of the dead, but of the living.*"

Afterward the Pharisees, rejoicing in the embarrassment of their hated rivals, the Sadducees, gathered again like barking wolves about a hunted quarry.

"Master," asked one of them hypocritically, "which is the great commandment in the law?" For, they argued, if we can but draw this witless carpenter's son into a discussion on the law we shall be able to put him to open shame before the multitude.

Jesus answered the scribe without hesitation, "The first commandment is, 'Hear, O Israel; The Lord our God, the Lord is one; and you shall love the Lord your God with all your heart, and with all your soul, and with all your mind, and with all your strength.' The second is this, 'You shall love your neighbor as thyself.' There is no other commandment greater than these."

He who had asked the question trembled under the searching eyes of the Nazarene. Suddenly, those familiar words of the temple ritual blazed within his darkened soul like a great light. And he answered truth with truth. "Master, you hath well said that he is one, and there is none other but he, and to love him with all the understanding, and with all the strength, and to love his neighbor as himself, is much more than all whole burnt offerings and sacrifices."

And Jesus said to this man, "You are not far from the kingdom of God." But upon the others, who were openly sneering at their spokesman and muttering anathemas in their great beards, he presently launched the most terrible words ever spoken to man. Ghastly woes upon woes reverberated in their astonished ears, while all the rottenness of their guilty hearts was suddenly torn open and laid bare for the rabble to gaze upon. "Serpents, offspring of vipers," he called them; and hissing, crawling, stinging, they crept away to their dens in murderous haste, while the fickle multitude, roused to a very frenzy of excitement, rocked and wept under the prophetic wail of his closing words, heavy with swift-approaching doom, "Oh Jerusalem, Jerusalem, which killed the prophets, and stoned them that are sent unto her! How often would I have gathered your children together, even as a hen gathers her chickens under her wings, and you would not! Behold, your house is left unto you desolate. For I say unto you, you shall not see me henceforth, till you shall say, 'Blessed is he that cometh in the name of the Lord.'"

And Judas, who had heard and saw all, staggered away, blind and crazed with anger and despair. "Ruin—ruin!" he muttered. "I see naught but black ruin! In his rash folly the man hath cut the last rope of safety. There is but one chance—one. He must again quell the storm he has raised about our ears with the word of his power, and I—yes, I will force him to it. I swear it!"

In that same hour the beggar, Tor, saw and heard what he has never forgotten to this moment of his eternity—nor yet will forget. Certain Greeks had come up to keep the Passover at Jerusalem, for they had abandoned the pagan rites of Rome and Athens, and were trying to serve the invisible Jehovah. These heard speedily of the new prophet who gathered the whole city to hear him in the temple, and they desired mightily to see him.

When one will see Jesus, even to this hour, his desire is granted to him. So then these Gentiles presently set their longing eyes upon the man they sought. And Jesus, looking with prophetic gaze down the vista of coming centuries, saw in these foreigners, with their clear, fair faces and candid eyes, those who should truly accept him as their King, understanding as the Jews could not the glories of his invisible kingdom. And seeing all that must be, he said to those about him, "The hour is come that the Son of man should be glorified."

And again he said, "Except a grain of wheat fall into the earth and die, it abideth by itself alone; but if it die, it beareth much fruit. He that loveth his life loseth it; and he that hateth his life in this world shall keep it unto life eternal. If any man serve me, let him follow me; and where I am, there shall also my servant be: if any man serve me, him will the Father honor. Now is my soul troubled; and what shall I say? Father, save me from this hour. But for this cause came I unto this hour. Father, glorify your name."

Then came a great Voice out of the unseen. "I have both glorified it, and will glorify it again."

The people heard the sound of the Voice and trembled. But not to every man is it given to hear aright; so some said, "It thundered," and rolled foolish eyes toward the cloudless heavens.

Others, awe-stricken, whispered, "An angel hath spoken to him."

To these Jesus spoke presently. "This voice hath not come for my sake, but for your sakes. Now is the judgment of this world: now shall the prince of this world be cast out. And I, if I be lifted up from the earth, will draw all men unto me."

Then one of the scribes, shaken out of his hypocrisy by the thunder of that celestial Voice, asked in all sincerity, "We have heard out of the law that the Christ abideth for ever, and how sayest you, The Son of man must be lifted up? Who is this Son of man?"

And Jesus, divinely patient, answered once again, "Yet a little while is the light among you. Walk while ye have the light, that darkness overtake ye not: and he that walkth in the darkness knowth not where he goeth. While ye have the light, believe on the light, that ye may become sons of light."

And with that word he went away and hid himself, and no man saw him for many hours.

Chapter 7
Felicia

Stronger even than the cords of love are the cords of habit. If a man has shaken a brazen cup and bellowed for alms for more than a score of years, the cup and the cry will have become a part of him, not lightly to be shaken off. Chelluh, with eyes, hungered as before, and as before he coveted money for his few and evil pleasures. So it came to pass that after a day spent in sight-seeing, he was again squatting comfortably in his familiar corner by the Damascus gate, his eyes closed, his bony knuckles beating a monotonous accompaniment to the familiar beggar's whine, "Have mercy, kind lords of Jerusalem! Have mercy on the sorrows of one born blind! Kind lords, beautiful ladies, only a denarius, I beseech of you!"

Tor, searching anxiously for his new Master in every corner of the city, came upon the beggar unawares, and stopped short in indignant amaze. "Did not the King, my Master, give you your sight only yesterday?" he demanded.

Chelluh opened his eyes with a muttered curse. "Who are you," he snarled, "to question me? How else shall I live?"

Tor looked hard at the man's great bulk. "There are many laborers working in the great quarries yonder," he answered slowly. "The Romans pay every man of them a silver penny."

Chelluh replied to this suggestion with a string of curses spoken in three languages. He ended by hurling a great stone at the lad's head. Badly aimed, the missile crashed over the wall of a garden nearby.

There was a moment of silence, during which Chelluh scuttled rapidly away. Then a small door in the wall was suddenly thrown open and two men darted out. They looked up and down the narrow street, and seeing no one but Tor, who stood staring in stupefied silence after the beggar, they seized the boy and dragged him into the enclosure, locking and barring the door behind them.

"'Tis an evil offspring of beggars that hath done this mischief," exclaimed one of the men angrily. "Did I not say it?"

The other man fixed his eyes on Tor. "Didst you throw the stone that broke the great vase yonder?" he asked.

Tor's wild, bright eyes followed the man's accusing finger to the spot where an urn carven from costly marble lay in ruins amid a tangle of bright flowers. "I did not throw the stone," he said.

"Lies!" cried the first man, stamping his foot. "Why question a dog? Give the fellow to me. I will scourge him soundly and thrust him forth. His bleeding back will, perchance, warn others of his sort to keep their distance from the palace."

"I am not a dog," said Tor boldly. "I am the servant of a King. I was looking for my Master, and another hurled the stone at me. But because the man was recently healed of blindness he could not throw a stone with ease, and therefore, it came over the wall."

One of the men shook with laughter at this speech. "Nay, but you are a pretty liar," he said at last. "The servant of a King! Aye, you dost look the part rarely! May I ask you the name of your royal Master?"

"His name is Jesus," said Tor. "I was blind, and he gave me eyes. Therefore, I serve him."

The faces of both men had grown suddenly serious. They exchanged significant glances. "Better hold the boy till my lord's return. He will, perchance, wish to question him on the matter," said one. And the other nodding, gripped the child roughly by the shoulder, and presently thrust him into an empty storage room of an inner court.

Tor flung himself against the heavy door in a sudden fury of despair. "Let me out!" he screamed. "Let me out! I must find my Master."

Then, as no one paid the slightest heed to his outcries, he began to look about him for some means of escape. The one window high in the wall was heavily barred, and there was no opening in the small, dark chamber except the door by which he had entered, and this was solidly locked on the outside.

The boy tore at his rags like a trapped animal. Then spying a great sealed jar in one corner he began to scratch savagely at its cover. "If it be wine," he muttered, "I will drink my fill for once. Nay, I will do more. I will spill upon the earth all that I cannot drink. I hate the men who have thrust me into this place! I also hate Chelluh. Some day I will kill him."

"Forgive, if ye have aught against any one, that your Father may forgive you."

Who had spoken? The beggar child ceased his beast-like clawing at the sealed lid of the jar. His flushed face paled slowly. "Forgive—forgive!" The words rang clearly in his bewildered ears. He sank slowly to the floor, and dropped his head to his lean knees in an effort to remember. "It was my Master who said it," he muttered at last. "He said 'Forgive, that your Father may forgive.' Father—my Father!"

The child's face lighted with sudden joy. "He said whosoever asks shall have. I will ask, for I want to get out of this place that I may follow my Master." Then in a loud, clear voice, after the fashion of the Pharisees he had heard praying in the temple and on the corners of the streets, he cried aloud, "Father, I want to get out of this place! My Father! I want to get out—Father! Father!"

There was a soft fumbling sound at the door. "Who is calling?" asked a sweet, imperious voice.

"I am calling," answered Tor expectantly. "I want to get out."

"I can't unlock the door," answered the voice, "but Oonah can. Be quiet till I fetch her."

A moment later the sunshine streamed in through the open door, revealing the figure of a very beautiful child on its threshold. Behind the child stood a young girl attired like a servant. She was smiling broadly. "How didst you come in here, boy?" She asked, staring curiously at the beggar's tear-stained face and scant rags.

"The fat man with the red tunic put me here," said Tor. "He said I broke the vase with a stone, but I did not."

"It was Marcus who shut him up," said the maid, pursing up her lips knowingly. "I must shut him in again, and make fast the door before Marcus finds out that I have opened it. Come, princess, we—"

"Be silent, Oonah, I wish to speak to the boy," said the child with a gesture of command. "Where is your father?" she continued, fixing her dark eyes on Tor. "I heard you calling him. I thought it was Set, the slave boy. He is always getting into trouble."

Tor pointed upward vaguely. "I called my Father who is in heaven," he said. "I have not seen him, but he causes what one asks to be done. My Master said so."

"Who said it?"

"My Master. His name is Jesus. He is a King. He made me see. I was blind."

"You were blind?" cried the serving-maid, laughing incredulously. "Nay, but thine eyes are bright as stars."

"They were not bright," said Tor soberly. "They were smitten into darkness. The Roman did it with his chariot-whip. But the King, my Master, touched them. So I see. I must find him. I pray you let me go!"

"Let him go," said the child imperiously. "Dost you hear me, Oonah? And, stay, I will give the boy my gold bracelet that father gave me yesterday."

The maid clasped her hands. "But, princess," she entreated, "what would the honorable lady, your mother, do with me if the bracelet is missing? Give to a beggar lad—for you see that he is nothing more. The boy would be scourged or stoned if found with such a jewel in his hand."

The child glanced doubtfully at Tor from under the curling black of her hair. "What shall I give you, boy?" she asked. "For I will give you something, you have amused me, and Oonah here is so stupid. I am quite weary of her."

"I am hungry," said Tor promptly. "Also, I am thirsty. Also, I want to get out of this place."

The little princess burst into a silvery laugh. "Come with me," she said imperiously. And, before the maid could stop her, she seized the beggar child by the hand and drew him away up the steps of a marble terrace. Oonah followed in terrified silence.

Beneath the shadow of a silken canopy, on a couch of ivory and silver cushioned with rose-colored damask reclined a lady. Tor thought that she was the most beautiful lady the sun had ever shone upon. The beggar's brilliant eyes sparkled with amazement and pleasure. His white teeth glimmered through his scarlet lips in an innocent smile, which faded before the look of haughty displeasure on the lady's fair face.

"What is this, Felicia?" she demanded, raising her head from the pillow to a white hand loaded with gems.

"Oh, my worshipful lady," began Oonah, trembling under the cold, questioning eyes which were bent upon her. "I beseech of you to listen to me, while I—"

"Be silent, Oonah," said Felicia, stamping her small foot. "I will explain. I was trying to amuse myself in the gardens, as usual, with this foolish Oonah," she went on rapidly, "and I heard someone call. It was this boy. That ugly, meddlesome Marcus had shut him into the cellar without food or drink. He has done nothing at all, and more than that he is the servant of a King. I wished to give him my bracelet and let him go. But Oonah disputed the matter with me, as I have forbidden her to do. May I not do as I will with my own?"

"Stay, my child, I will call Marcus," said the lady, smiling. "He will explain."

"Nay, he shall not interfere," cried the spoiled child. "The boy hath amused me, and Marcus shall not have him. This Jerusalem is so dull. I am weary of it." The child threw back her head with an exaggerated gesture of apathy which brought another smile to the lady's lips.

"How hath the boy amused you, little one!" she asked languidly. "If there is anything diverting about this place I would fain hear of it."

"The boy was blind, Mother, and the King, his Master, touched his eyes and they became bright, as you see them. Is not that an amusing story?"

"What King in Jerusalem can heal blind eyes?" asked the lady, turning with some curiosity to Tor.

"His name is Jesus," said Tor simply.

The lady drew her delicate brows together. "I have heard of the man," she said coldly. "He is arousing rebellion among the turbulent Jews, as hath many before him. He will shortly be dealt with after his kind, I doubt not."

"He will not be hurt," said Tor positively. "My Father will not permit anything to befall him."

"Your Father?" repeated the lady. "And who, pray, is your Father?"

"He is in heaven," explained Tor. "He listens to me, and to anyone who calls. It was because I prayed to him, as my Master said, that the door was opened. And now, let me go. I must find my Master."

"Stay," said the lady frowning, "I will be further amused. Were you always blind—before the King, your Master, touched you?"

"No," said Tor. "I had my eyes as now. Then one day I pursued the Roman Pilate, as he rode in his chariot, and asked for denarii. He struck me with his whip, and the lash blinded me. I cursed the man many times in my blindness with strong curses that blight like a flame. But now I have forgiven him, because my Master commands me to forgive if I have aught against any one. I have forgiven the cruel Gentile, who is hated in all of Jerusalem. I have also forgiven—"

Tor was interrupted by a smothered exclamation from the lady. Her dark eyes were blazing with sudden anger. "Take him away," she commanded. "Thrust him into the street—at once. Dost you hear, Oonah!"

The child, Felicia, stood as if rooted to the ground in amazement, her large eyes brimming over with tears, while Oonah, roused to action by the wrath in her mistress's face, seized Tor by the shoulder and hurried him through the garden, pausing only to unlock a small door in the wall.

"Run, now, beggar, for your wretched life," whispered the girl, as she pushed the boy into the street. "This is the house of Pilate, and yonder was his wife and child."

Chapter 8
Chelluh Drives a Bargain

The dog, Baladan, led a lonely life in these days. Confined to his own little quarter of Jerusalem by that unwritten yet pitiless law which prevails to this day among the half wild street dogs of oriental cities, he dared not follow his adopted master beyond the corner of the short, dark street which was his chosen haunt. After some mysterious fashion the dog was aware that if he should he venture alone into the streets and squares beyond he would be instantly torn in pieces.

'Tis seldom that an animal of the outcast breed shows the least regard or affection for men. But Tor was so like a little animal himself that the heart of the great, gaunt beast had gone out to him. And Tor responded in kind. The undivided love of a beast is better than no love at all. Perhaps it is because of this that the heart of a dog is so loving. More than once it has solaced pain that would otherwise be unbearable in the nobler heart of a child.

Baladan was licking with anxious care a fragment of leather once worn by his little master. This done, he laid his ugly head upon it, and dreamed a vague dream of delight in which one figure—the figure of Tor—moved always before him.

Suddenly he sprang up, his rough coat bristling, and listened, then with a whine of delight bounded forward and flung himself upon the small, half-naked figure that was stealing along in the shadow of the high walls.

Tor was breathing fast and his puny chest heaved with an occasional strangling sob as he flung himself down by the dog. "Oh, Baladan," he whispered, "I can't find him. What shall I do?"

Baladan covered the child's feet with warm, wet kisses, his great yellow-brown eyes brimming over with tears of anxious affection. He moaned and gurgled and laid one hard paw on his master's knee in token of his utter allegiance. Tor wound his thin arms about the dog's neck, and buried his face in the scanty yellow fur. "Let us sleep, Baladan," he said drowsily, after a time. And the two curled themselves in their old haunt under the dark archway and presently dreamed and slept.

The sound of voices lowered to a hissing whisper suddenly aroused the child. He touched the dog warningly, and listened. A name had been spoken— the name of his Master—he was sure of it.

"I have a score to settle with the Galilean, I tell you," said the whining voice of Chelluh. "The other man is nothing to me."

"Did he not heal you of blindness?" demanded the second voice with a touch of impatience.

"He did, and that I will swear to. Since then the matter has been noised abroad, and no one will give me so much as a denarius to buy my daily meals. They tell me to work—to dig—to cut stone—to build walls. May the Furies* reward them! I will not work, and I will eat."

"You shalt eat your fill if you wilt do my bidding. Listen. This man, Jesus, who has so taken your living from you, is either a God or a false prophet— may Jehovah help me, but I know not what he is! The priests and Pharisees hate him. The people are divided. He must declare himself either one way or the other. I have sworn that I will force him to it. And I have sworn further to deliver him into the hands of the priests without tumult. I have watched you and you are a tool fitted to my hand. Go you among those of thine own sort and arouse them against the man. You canst do it. You hast a nimble tongue, and the rabble will hear you."

"What if he be a god," demanded Chelluh, with a gesture of fear. "Nay, I will have none of it. He opened mine eyes, and I was born blind. I am afraid to lift my hand against such a man."

"But if he is a god," said the other eagerly, "he will make it known rather than die like a criminal. Hark you, they will stone him, or crucify him, if they are able."

"I am afraid of the man," growled Chelluh. "And who are you to do this thing? I am no whining Levite, but you—are verily a devil."

"I am a patriot," declared the other boldly. "I know the man well. He professes to be Messiah. If

* In Greek and Roman mythology three spirits of vengeance.

he is the true Deliverer, not a hair of his head shall be hurt, if not, let him die the death. I have sworn it."

Then was a short silence broken by the musical chink of silver. "There is naught to fear from Jesus of Nazareth," said the voice of the man who had declared himself a patriot. "He would render to no man evil for evil. I have heard him say it many times, and I know that he is true. He loves his enemies and forgives every one who offends—not once only, but seventy times seven. If he prove to be the Messiah I shall confess my plans and my thoughts to him, and he will forgive me readily. I shall then be a great prince and have power in the new kingdom. This paltry sum shall be multiplied to you thrice over."

"I will do it," said Chelluh, shaking the silver pieces in his hard palms till they chinked again. "And I also will be forgiven, after I have worked my will with the man and with the multitude." The beggar laughed aloud.

Tor shuddered at the evil sound as he lay quiet in his lair. After that the silence remained unbroken, and the child at length ventured to peep out from the archway. The two men were just emerging into the brightly-lighted square beyond, and the sun falling full upon the face of Chelluh's companion revealed it as the face of Judas. Tor flung his arms about the neck of the dog. "Oh, Baladan," he whispered, "I must find my Master. If I were only a great man with a great sword how I would fight for him!"

But the boy remained where he was for another hour till the sun had sunken behind the mountains. Then, emerging into the twilight of the narrow street, he trotted noiselessly away. Baladan followed at his heels like a shadow, and like a shadow refused to be left behind at the accustomed boundary. Some vague stirring in the dog's loving heart told him that his master was going into danger, and forthwith his own imminent peril was forgotten.

To his unbounded joy, Tor saw not many rods distant the figure of Peter, the Galilean, walking swiftly along with bent head. He ran to him and, placing himself directly in the man's way, bowed himself humbly before him. "I beseech you to listen to me, honorable Galilean," he began, "for I have evil tidings which concern my Master."

The dog whined uneasily, and flattened his lean body against the stones. The man's angry eyes cut him like a lash.

"Out of my way," said the Galilean, with profound disgust. "What hast you to do with the Master?"

He strode forward, shaking off with a shudder of loathing the small imploring hand of the beggar child. "They will kill him," cried Tor. "The man said so. They hate him!"

The dog sprang forward with a low growl of anger and fastened his white teeth in the garments of the fisherman. That wail of anguish in his master's voice had roused him to a frenzy.

The Galilean in a rage raised his stout oaken staff and threw the animal against the wall. He meant only to free himself from the animal but the gaunt body quivered, dropped, rolled over once, and was still.

The Jew hurried away, breathing deep in his anger and disgust at his own rage. "I am defiled," he muttered, "for the breath of an unclean beast hath polluted my garments." He glanced back over his shoulder and beheld the beggar kneeling by the body of the dog.

That same night the Passover was sacrificed, and all Jerusalem feasted with solemn rites and decorous rejoicings. But Tor crouched on the stones outside one of the low, dark houses within the third wall of the city. He had followed the Galilean afar off, had seen him at length with his Master and the twelve enter this house. The child dozed off and on as the hours passed, and the white moon looked down at him between the houses. He had forgiven Peter, the Galilean, for the death of Baladan, even as his Master had commanded, and that singular peace which the world neither gives nor takes away filled his soul.

He could have told no man why he was so strangely content, when, in the old days, fury would have scorched him. For the moment he had forgotten the evil words of Chelluh and the disciple called Judas. Remembering them, he murmured a simple prayer to the mysterious, unseen Father, in whom he was coming to believe with all the strength of his childish being. "Our Father will take care of my Master," he said aloud, and smiled alone in the darkness.

Within the house, in a large upper chamber, Jesus sat at his last meal upon earth with the few whom he had chosen, knowing all things that should shortly come to pass, and understanding to the full the pitiful ignorance and darkness in the hearts of the disciples.

Again they disputed among themselves as to which of them should be accounted greatest in that coming kingdom of glory which the Master now told them plainly had been appointed unto him. To sit upon twelve thrones judging the twelve tribes of Israel was, indeed, a glorious future. They accepted the idea with pleasure, but one must be greater than his fellows in any kingdom, and each of them coveted the supreme crown of power.

Then Jesus, knowing that the Father had given all things into his hands, and that he came forth from God, and was going to God, arose from supper, and laying aside his garments, took a basin and began to wash the disciples' feet, and to wipe them with the towel wherewith he was girded. And so he came in turn to Peter.

Peter said to him, "Lord, you shalt never wash my feet."

Jesus answered, "If I wash you not, you hast no part with me."

"Lord, not my feet only," said Peter, "but my hands and my head."

Then came that dark moment when the man called Judas received the morsel of bread dipped in wine. "What you doest, do quickly," said the Master, with a look of full understanding which penetrated the dismal labyrinth of the man's soul like a flash of blinding light.

Judas ran violently out of the house, and the darkness swallowed him. He knew himself at last. He was no eager patriot, no doubting disciple, anxious to force a triumphant issue. He ground his teeth in a very fury of rage and hatred, as he sped on his terrible mission.

The beggar child, dozing on the cold stones outside, shuddered at sound of that ominous, hurrying footfall. "My Father will take care of him," he murmured, and again slept.

Within that dimly-lighted upper chamber the compassionate Master was trying to prepare the little company of unsuspecting disciples for the darker hours just before them. "All ye shall be offended because of me this night," he said sorrowfully. "For it is written, I will strike the shepherd, and the sheep of the flock shall be scattered abroad. But after I am raised up, I will go before you into Galilee."

Peter answered in his bold, positive way, "Although all others shall be offended, yet will not I."

Jesus said to him, "Verily, I say unto you, that this night, before the cock crows twice, you shall deny me three times."

But the Galilean answered with exceeding vehemence, "If I must die with you, I will not deny you!"

And so likewise said all the others.

Chapter 9
Before the Cock Crows

The promise of solitude led the man Christ Jesus to Gethsemane in his darkest hour. And there under the dense shadow of the ancient olives he threw himself down upon the ground for that last exceeding bitter struggle with his humanity.

And Peter, the Galilean, and the others—slept.

Tor had followed them, noiseless and unseen as a friendly shadow. He did not approach the King, his Master, nor did he again venture to accost Peter. Squatting motionless at the gate of the garden, the child thought confusedly but joyfully of his deliverance from the house of Pilate.

"It was because I prayed to my Father," he told himself, and hugged his lean little body with a low laugh of pleasure. "Hereafter I need fear nothing. I will call and he will deliver me, and neither man nor demon can hinder him."

His soul went out in a flood of love toward the Man who had opened his eyes, and who was at that moment lying upon his face under the olives in agony, and the child's pure thoughts mingled with the thoughts of angels which comforted him.

Somewhere, afar off, lights gleamed among the dark trees. Stealthy footsteps and hushed voices beyond the garden wall readied the boy's keen ears. He sprang up and listened intently.

The glare of smoking torches and the irregular tread of hurrying feet sent vibrations of horror through the shuddering night. But the Man of Nazareth no longer lay upon his face amid the shadows. He came forth to receive the brimming cup of his sorrows radiant with the power that had never failed him. Stooping over his sleeping disciples he called them, "Arise, let us be going. Behold, he that betrayeth me is at hand."

Now Judas had before agreed with the officers that he would greet his Master with a kiss. "So that ye may know the man from his disciples—stupid fellows every one and not worth the taking."

As the motley crowd of temple police, bearing torches, followed by a rabble of the curious, advanced into the gloom of the garden a superstitious awe fell upon them. They drew back and hesitated, casting fearful glances at the dark masses of trees moving gently in the night wind. Some unseen, noiseless terror seemed to lurk amid the shifting shadows. "If the man be a prophet," whispered one, "there will be blasting lightnings at his call. Let us go back."

But Judas turned his sneering face upon the speaker with a low laugh of scorn. "Master! Master!" he cried mockingly, and running forward he clasped and kissed the Savior of the world.

Jesus said to him, "Judas, do you betray the Son of man with a kiss?"

"Lord, shall we strike with the sword?" cried one of the disciples.

Not waiting for an answer, Peter drew his weapon and aimed a mighty blow at the man nearest him. The man fell back with a bellow of rage and pain, while his companions sprang forward and seized Jesus.

The eyes of the prisoner, grave, calm, and compassionate, were fixed upon the wounded man, from whose severed ear blood spurted in a torrent. "Permit me please," he said gently to the officers who grasped him by the arms, and reaching forth he touched the ear and healed it.

Then that omniscient gaze turned full upon Peter, who stood staring in a frozen stupor at the being he had believed to be the invincible Messiah.

"Put up again your sword into its place," said the Master; "for all who live by the sword shall perish with the sword." Then, answering further the thoughts that looked out of the bewildered, terror-stricken eyes of the man whom he had named "The Rock," he said, "Thinkest you that I cannot now pray to my Father, and he shall presently give me more than twelve legions of angels? But how then shall the scriptures be fulfilled, that thus it must be?"

But he uttered no prayer to his Father, and the ranks of the angelic host remained hidden from the expectant eyes that searched the empty heavens.

In that same hour Jesus said to the multitude which gathered about him, threatening, yet awe-stricken by the miracle, "Have ye come out as against a thief, with swords and clubs? When I was daily with ye in the temple, ye stretched forth no hands against me, but this is your hour, and the power of darkness."

At that word the darkness closed in about him—and it was night.

In the courtyard of the high priest's house Tor lurked in the shelter of a doorway and looked on. No one had noticed the child as he slipped in with the crowd that held at its core the silent Man of Nazareth. Peter had also followed. Tor watched the Galilean seat himself with the others at a small fire which was kindled in the midst of the place. He had turned his back upon the travesty of a legal examination which was going on at the upper end of the hall and was warming his fingers with an air of complete indifference.

"So the dangerous Prophet is proven but a man of straw, after all," quoted one of the lesser officers of the police with a contemptuous gesture toward the meek figure of the Nazarene. "Look upon the fellow now. He hath never a word to say for himself, and there are no lightnings—no thunders. By the seven-branched candlestick, I declare to you that I was in a cold sweat when I laid hands on the man. But I felt nothing more terrible than an arm of flesh and blood under his rabbi's robe."

"A rabbi's robe, indeed," chuckled another. "He will wear another sort before many days, I promise you."

"But what sayest you to the healing of Malchus' ear?" demanded a woman who had approached the fire. "He declares that from this time on he is a believer."

A great shout of laughter greeted this speech. "Malchus hath ever a nimble tongue," quoth a black-bearded young fellow who carried a short sword stuck in his belt. "A nimble tongue, say I, and the long ears of a donkey. One of the Galileans made a lunge at him, but, being a clumsy knave of a fisherman and knowing naught of the uses of a sword, he merely grazed the ear."

"Nay, fellow, the ear was sliced clean off," growled Peter, stung to retort by the sneering words of the Judean.

The woman bent forward to stare at the speaker. "Art ye also one of the man's disciples?" she asked curiously.

"I am not," said Peter shortly. He was listening painfully to his Master's voice in low-toned response to a question of the high priest. At sound of a violent, flat-handed blow, he twisted about, in his place and beheld the colorless face of Jesus slowly reddening under the insult. "If I have spoken evil," he was saying in a low, clear voice, "bear witness of the evil, but if well, why do you strike me?"

The Galilean rose from his place at the fire, breathing deep, his strong hands clenched at his sides in futile anger. "Why does he not blast them with the word of his power?" he asked himself as he stealthily watched the terrible mockery of justice which was now drawing to its close.

They were questioning the prisoner sharply now. Peter could see the dark looks of satisfaction on the faces of the priests and Sanhedrins and the sneering laughter of the rabble at their back. Then came a show of witnesses against the prisoner. Among the witnesses stood Chelluh, the beggar who had once been blind.

"The man healed me of blindness—yes, it is so, most worshipful lords," he whined. "It was accomplished by black magic and the power of Beelzebub, I declare to you, for he who would destroy the temple of God must needs be of the devil."

"What are ye saying of the temple, fellow?" demanded the high priest. "Did the man dare to threaten the temple?"

"Most holy and reverend high priest," replied Chelluh, "the Nazarene said in my hearing, and in the hearing of this friend of mine—an honest craftsman, as you see, 'I am able to destroy the temple of God, and to build it in three days!'"

The high priest arose in his place and fixed his eyes upon the prisoner. "Do you answer nothing?" he hissed between set teeth. "What is the meaning of this saying which these reputable witnesses bring against you?"

Jesus seemed not to have heard the question. His inscrutable eyes were bent upon the ground. Upon his face shone a faint, mysterious light. The high priest bent forward and stared at him, unrelentingly. "I command you by the living God, that you tell us whether you be the Christ, the Son of God!" he cried in a terrible voice.

The Man of Nazareth lifted his meek head at that word. "I am," he said slowly—distinctly. "And ye shall see the Son of man sitting at the right hand of power, and coming with the clouds of heaven."

"He hath spoken blasphemy!" exclaimed the high priest, tearing his garments with a gesture of outraged holiness. "What further need have we of witnesses? Ye have heard the blasphemy! What do ye think?"

"Death—death! He is guilty!" came the deep-throated answer of the priests.

Cries of triumph, dreadful laughter, the sound of buffeting palms burst forth from judges and witnesses alike. Someone blindfolded him. Then some hit him.

"Prophesy unto us, you Christ. Who is he that smote you?" yelled the savage voice of the beggar who had received his sight, and he smote his blinded Savior with open palms twice—thrice—many times.

A suffocating mist rolled blood-red before the eyes of Peter. "If he were the Messiah," he groaned, "this could not be. The man must have mocked and deceived us from the beginning!"

Somewhere, not far away, sounded the cheerful crowing of a rooster. "I will go back to Galilee," he muttered. But his leaden feet carried him no farther from the awful scene than the porch. Here he loitered, listening with a frightful, strained attention to the sounds of coarse talking and laughter that came out to him through the half-open doors. "I will go," he said aloud. "I must go. It is already day."

The servants of the high priest's household were astir and cheerfully busy with their morning tasks. One of them, a buxom maid bearing a jar upon her head, paused and stared attentively at the Galilean. "Aha!" she exclaimed. "This man also was with Jesus, the Nazarene."

Peter raised his heavy eyes to the fresh-colored, inquisitive face of the woman. "I know not the man," he snarled with an oath. The woman went her way with a laughing gesture of unbelief.

Then others of the bystanders began to cast curious glances at the haggard face and wild eyes of the stranger. They whispered among themselves for a space, then a man wearing the uniform of the house of Annas advanced with an air of determination. "Certainly, you art one of them," he said authoritatively, "for you art a Galilean."

Peter turned upon the man with a torrent of angry oaths. "I tell you, fellow," he cried loudly, "that I know not this man of whom you speak."

The rooster crowed for the second time.

The great doors of the judgment-hall were flung wide, and the motley throng of priests and underlings, glutted with their awful triumph, pushed through, dragging the piteous figure of their prisoner. The face of the Nazarene gleamed white and calm amid the dark looks of his persecutors. His loving eyes turned for the last time upon Peter and flashed into his darkened soul the remembrance of that sad word of prophecy, "Before the cock crows twice, you shall deny me three times."

And Peter went out and wept bitterly.

Chapter 10
In the Palace Garden

T he wife of Pilate arose from her couch with a troubled and haggard look on her fair face. The maid who attended the great lady's dressing table observed this with curiosity. "There is tumult about the gates of the palace this morning," she said, as she combed out the long black tresses with a comb of gold and ivory, preparatory to weaving them into a graceful crown of braided strands.

The princess shrugged her fair shoulders with a slight gesture of weariness. "There is always tumult," she said languidly. "Ah me, 'tis a dreary place—this Jerusalem. I wish I were once again safely at Rome."

"If my noble lady will but glance into the mirror, she will behold a fairer sight than even Rome can offer," said the maid submissively, and skillfully fastened a fresh-blown rose so that its crimson petals rested on the graceful neck of her mistress. "But the tumult of this morning differs from that of other days, honorable princess," she went on eagerly. "Diomed says that the Jews have seized their prophet and are about to put him to death—if, indeed, they are allowed."

"What prophet, girl?" demanded the lady, a faint flush stealing into her pale cheeks. "Every man is a prophet—or a priest, is it not so, in this hateful Jerusalem? And the prophets have loud voices, and they are always creating a tumult."

"I myself have seen this man," said the girl. "He is quite unlike the other rabbis, as they call them—of a gentle voice, and a stature majestic. I think of my gods in Athens. Yet this man is a Jew."

"His name?"

"His name is Jesus, but they also call him the Nazarene."

The princess uttered a faint exclamation.

"Pardon me, I beseech you, honorable mistress, if I have fastened that last plait too tightly," hastily interposed the maid, withdrawing a jeweled pin from its place and readjusting it with elaborate care.

"Did you say they were bringing the Nazarene here—to the palace?" demanded the princess, turning her large dark eyes upon her servant.

"Honorable lady, the man is already here, and my lord, the governor, is attending the case upon the seat of judgment. The Jews refused to wait for the proper hour, and my lord Pilate, with his usual indulgence, came forth to them. These barbarians have no hearts, noble lady, they are without consideration for the sleep of an illustrious Roman. They should be scourged as slaves."

"What will they do with him?" muttered the wife of Pilate, clenching her white hands. "Nay, my lord should have nothing to do with this prophet. He must dismiss the case."

The maid stared at her mistress in some perplexity. "The morning is warm and fair," she said at last. "Will it please your highness to breakfast upon the terrace? The lady Felicia is already playing in the garden of the inner court."

In the secluded spot where slaves had spread a table with the breakfast-service of the princess, the morning sun struck sparks of splendor from burnished plates and crystal, gem-rimmed goblets. Flowers of every delicate color and odor, violets from Gethsemane, lilies from the deep vale of Kidron, roses from the nearer gardens of the palace, heaped a golden bowl in the center, while around it glowed the richer hues of fruit, brought from distant parts of the country, and flagons of delicate wine, cooling in beds of snow fetched from the crown of Lebanon for this spoiled daughter of Rome.

The lady cast a dissatisfied glance about the garden. "Where is Felicia?" she asked sharply.

"She was here but a moment ago, noble lady," replied the maid, who had followed her mistress with a fan of peacock's feathers and an armful of embroidered pillows. "I will call Oonah."

But neither Oonah nor the child were anywhere to be found, and after a little while the princess began her meal with frowning brows. "There is too much noise about the place," she observed in a displeased tone, as she tasted a silver fig smothered in wine and spices.

The servants glanced at one another with lifted brows. "It cannot be helped, honorable mistress," ventured one of them, a young Greek lad, beautiful as a creation of Praxiteles* in his short tunic bordered with blue, "All the loud mouthed Jews of the city, it would seem, headed by their priests, are surrounding the judgment-seat before the palace. The guard would not have admitted them, but my lord, the governor, ordered it."

"He could not do otherwise," said the lady, with a slight curl of her haughty lip. "But what is it that they are saying over and again? 'Tis a horrid sound, like the cry of wolves hungering after their prey."

Again the servants exchanged half-frightened glances, and again the handsome young Greek answered his lady. "'Tis a custom in this Jerusalem for the governor to release a prisoner at feast time," he said in a low voice. "Perchance, the people are demanding this pledge from the illustrious Pilate."

The lady's face cleared. "Ah, it is so," she cried, "I remember how it befell last year. My lord will release to them the Nazarene, who is called Jesus. Is it not so, Diomed?"

The Greek hesitated, and in the moment of silence the child, Felicia, closely followed by her nurse, rushed into the garden. Her dark hair was disordered, and her brown eyes reddened with angry tears. "They shall not scourge the boy!" she cried, stamping her small foot. "I have said it, but that stupid, wicked Marcus declares that he will do it. Wilt you not send for him, Mother and cause him to be punished for disobeying me?"

The princess turned her eyes severely upon Oonah. "Where hath the child been, and what is all this about Marcus? What has happened?"

* A famous Greek sculptor

Oonah trembled under the cold looks of her mistress. "'Tis the beggar boy again," she faltered. "He was beating upon the door of the outer court like a mad thing, and demanding speech with your highness. But, of course, Marcus—"

"Marcus is a beast—an animal!" again interrupted Felicia passionately. "Listen to me, I can explain everything far better than this stupid Oonah. Do you not remember the beggar lad whose eyes were restored by a King named Jesus? I brought him to this very spot two or three days ago. The boy amused me with his story. But Oonah thrust him forth because—"

"I remember," said the wife of Pilate with a strange look. "What then?"

"The mob wishes to kill his Master, the King, and the lad came hither to beg for his life. Marcus was about to scourge him and thrust him forth, but I forbade it. I say he shall not harm the boy. Do command it also, my mother—and quickly, for Marcus will not obey me."

"Fetch the lad to me, Diomed," ordered the lady briefly.

The young Greek obeyed, and presently returned to the presence of his mistress followed by the irate porter, his big hand buried in the rough curls of the beggar's head. Tor presented a pitiable appearance, his pallid face streaked with tears and dust, his great eyes wide with fear and horror.

At sight of the princess the child fell sobbing to his knees and lifted his lean arms in an agony of petition. "My Master—my Master!" he wailed. And again, "My Master, oh, my Master!"

76

The wife of Pilate signed to Marcus to release the boy, then she ordered Diomed to give him wine.

Tor obediently swallowed from the cup which was held to his lips, but not once did he remove his beseeching eyes from the beautiful haughty face of the princess. "You can save him," he whispered.

The lady shook her head. "I fear that I cannot," she said. Then to the astonishment of every one present she laid her delicate hand on the beggar's rough head. "Tell me why you love this man—this Nazarene?" she asked softly. "Nay, do not weep and tremble so, child. I will do all that I can to save him."

Tor choked back his tears and gazed steadfastly into the exquisite troubled face which leaned toward him. "I love him—because he loves—me," he faltered. "He opened my eyes. he is good. He is the King—my Master. I love him."

"Why do the Jews hate him so?" murmured the lady. "In my dream I saw him—as one altogether lovely, enthroned high above all the gods of Rome and Greece. Then I saw—" She broke off with a shudder. The wild tumult of voices in the square without had risen into an awful, insistent iteration of one terrible phrase.

"What do they say now?" she demanded with slowly-whitening face, turning to Diomed, who watched the scene with a satirical curl of his handsome lips.

"They are demanding the crucifixion of some criminal, your noble highness," replied the Greek, smirking courtier-like. "But why trouble thyself, dear princess, over the doings of the wild rabble?

The man, Jesus, is no more than a Jewish peasant—a carpenter, they say. What can such a one be to the fairest princess in—"

"Go, see what is happening without," ordered the lady, with a look which froze the insolent smile on the lips of the Greek. "Go, and return quickly."

The Greek reappeared almost immediately with a white, scared face. "The scene without is beyond description, noble lady," he began hurriedly, answering the command in the eyes of his mistress. "The whole city is at the doors demanding the crucifixion of the Nazarene. The most noble Pilate believes him innocent of any crime, and would save him if possible, but—hear the mob!"

It was impossible to hear anything else. Those awful beast-like cries penetrated the ears of the very slaves so that they cowered and trembled. "My tablets, Maia," whispered the wife of Pilate. With shaking fingers she wrote a few words upon the wax. "Take this," she said, turning to the Greek, "and give it into the hand of Pilate himself—no other. Go quickly!"

The Greek drew back in manifest terror. "What, art you afraid?" sneered the princess. "Stop, I will go myself. Perhaps I can save him." She arose and was descending the steps of the terrace, when the child Felicia flung herself at her mother's knees with a scream of terror. "Do not go out into that dreadful place, Mother," begged the child. "They are horrible—those Jews. Stay with me!"

The princess paused, hesitated, and finally yielded the tablets into the outstretched hand of Diomed. "Go—quickly!" she urged.

Chapter 11
Love Triumphant

To Pilate, governor of Jerusalem, seated upon the ivory chair of office before the palace, came the message from his wife. He glanced down at it with some impatience, when Diomed thrust the tablets into his hand with a hurried word of explanation.

"Have nothing to do with that righteous man," he read, "for I have suffered many things this day in a dream because of him."

The message was signed and sealed with the signet of the Roman princess. Pilate's pallid and heavy face whitened to the lifeless hues of the wax upon which the fateful words were written. Before him stood the drooping but still majestic figure of the Nazarene, robed in the purple robe of his torture and wearing the crown of thorns, a piteous sight, before which angels were veiling their shamed faces. Beyond the soldiers of the Roman guard surged the wildest, cruelest mob of all the ages.

The governor rose to his feet slowly, and, advancing to the side of the prisoner, exclaimed in his loud, passionless voice, "Behold the man!"

Mocking laughter, furious incoherent shouts, coupled with the dreadful, insistent, "Crucify him! Crucify him!" burst out in wilder clamor.

Pilate looked forth over the sea of terrible upturned eyes, and his huge limbs trembled beneath him. Again he glanced at the pale, melancholy face of the prisoner. "The fellow is naught but a Jewish peasant," he assured himself. "And after all, what use to cast Roman justice before dogs. They will have none of it." Loudly he called for water in a basin, and in sight of them all washed his hands with spectacular solemnity, saying, "I am innocent of the blood of this just person, see ye to it!"

Back came the mocking, inhuman cry, "His blood be upon us and upon our children!"

Pilate ground his teeth in impotent rage, and, seizing Jesus roughly by the shoulder, he thrust him forward in the face of the mob. "Shall I crucify your King?" he shouted derisively.

"We have no king but Caesar!" was the blasphemous answer. And with that word was the scroll rolled up and sealed with the seven seals of wrath against the day of wrath.

And they took Jesus and led him away.

On that same day Tor was again a prisoner. The wife of Pilate in real pity had commanded that the child should be comfortably entertained in the servants' quarters until all should be over.

Diomed, to whom the carrying out of this commission was entrusted, spoke softly to the beggar in the presence of his mistress, bidding him follow. Out of sight of the lady the Greek laughed aloud in his scorn. "Here is a guest for our honorable entertainment," he said to the chief butler. "My lady the princess hath commanded it. In which of the chambers of state shall I lodge my lord?" The official sniffed his disdain. "Is it an animal?" he demanded.

"It is an animal, most wise Clodius," laughed Diomed. "A Jewish swine—eh?—albeit a small one. Give him food and wine, excellent Clodius, for he is chiefly bone—this animal."

Tor ate, for he was starving. He also slept fitfully, for he was exhausted with fear and weeping. The sun shone warm and friendly from the cloudless spring heavens, and the child, lying upon a rug which one of the slaves had flung down for him, drowsily watched the ceaseless dance of young grape leaves in the soft warm wind.

The tumult without had suddenly ceased, and an ominous silence lay heavily upon the city. Tor thought lovingly of his Master in the intervals between dreams. "He has gone away safely with the men," he told himself. "I shall again find him, and he will heal blind folk as before." So dozing and murmuring soft prayers to his invisible Father, the beggar child rested in the house of Pilate, while without the walls of the city his Master, the King, was already hanging upon the cross.

Within the great kitchens of the palace cooks were busy preparing the noonday meal. Dishes and cups clattered cheerfully, and the merry voices of maidens burnishing the great wine-bottles mingled with the chirp and whir of sparrows flitting back and forth in the blue air.

Suddenly, and without warning, the bright light of the spring noon began to fail. There was no fog, no storm, but a veil of lurid darkness was drawn heavily across the sky. Doors and windows were thrown wide, and terror-stricken faces stared up into the threatening heavens.

Marcus, the crusty porter of the palace, stood fast in his place, his dull face blanched and terrified in the failing light. "'Tis the vengeance of the gods," he muttered. "The Man of Nazareth was innocent!"

Servants and underlings crowded the passages in terrified groups. "Open to us, Marcus," they cried, beating upon the doors till they trembled upon their heavy hinges. "Earthquake!" wailed a voice from without. "The gods are shaking this evil city!"

The porter drew the great bolts with tremulous haste, and with one accord all rushed into the street.

Scarcely knowing how it had befallen, the beggar child found himself on the street with the others, running—running he knew not whither, through empty streets which echoed his light footfalls as in the dead of night.

Somewhere, afar off, there was the tumult of a great multitude. Tor stopped to listen, then ran on, thinking of his Master, who was waiting for him in the fast-gathering darkness.

He reached a gate—which gate he knew not, but it yawned wide and unguarded. Not far away Tor could hear the frightened sobbing of women, the strong curses of terrified men, the wailing of little children, blending with the hurried trampling of myriad feet. Suddenly across the darkness flamed a blood-red, silent flash illuminating the heavens from east to west. Against this lurid background loomed three crosses, stark and black. And now across the gloomy valleys sounded the sullen crash of rocks, the fall of giant trees, while the sick earth groaned aloud and trembled beneath its terrible burden.

Tor stood stock-still in the midst of the road. In that instant of frozen horror he comprehended what had happened. "Oh, my Father," he groaned, the foundations of his childish faith reeling with the reeling earth.

And the Omnipotent Love answered this feeble cry of the least of his children, even as it answered that far-reaching, agonized appeal which was sounding forth from Calvary. And so in a moment—or an eternity—the heavens cleared and the spring sun shone brightly upon the crosses with their piteous burdens, upon the terror-stricken multitudes returning to doomed Jerusalem, upon open tombs and shattered mountains, upon a little child, comforted by his Father, gazing with Christ-touched eyes upon the cross of his King.

They took away the body of Jesus before sunset, wrapping it in fine white linen and odorous spices, and laying it to rest in a garden near by. Tor watched all, understanding little of the significance of the rock-hewn tomb, of the great stone before its door, of the Roman guard which was shortly stationed before the sealed sepulcher.

When all was finished the child returned to the city, sustained by some strange expectation which he could have explained to no one. As he would have entered the gate he came upon a woeful figure standing without and beating upon its breast. It was Chelluh, his wicked face disfigured with rage and pain. "My eyes," he groaned. "The sight of that accursed cross burnt them like a devouring flame." And so it was. And so will it ever be. He who can look upon that cross of agony without tears of love and pity, henceforth sees only the blackness of darkness. The eyes of his soul are withered.

Tor led the blind man to his old place by the gate, and fetched him his cup, his staff, and his water-gourd.

"Now go, little dog, buy me oil and wine," cried the beggar, with one of his frightful maledictions, "and return to me quickly, for I am devoured with this flame."

But Tor, looking upon him sorrowfully, knew that he could no more serve this evil master as in the old days. "I have helped you this much," he said in his clear childish voice, "because of the King, my Master, and because of my Father in heaven. But I can no longer abide in your presence. Farewell!" And with this he was gone, his naked feet making no sound upon the stones of the street.

Many days thereafter did Chelluh send forth his dolorous cry for alms in the doomed city of Jerusalem, for he lived until the terrible days of the Roman siege, perishing at last of hunger in his chosen place by the Damascus gate.

In the green garden, near Calvary, where the Roman guards paced ceaselessly back and forth before that silent tomb, Tor lingered, unnoticed and unafraid as the birds that flitted among the branches of the blossoming trees. It comforted him to be near the resting-place of his Master; and the lusty life of the young summer sent vague thrills of expectancy through his brown limbs, as he lay upon the warm earth watching the shifting leaf-shadows playing upon the sealed door of the sepulcher, and the slow-moving figures of the guards clad in the scarlet and gold of imperial Rome.

Toward midnight of the second night, when the great Passover moon rode high in the heavens and the garden slept in its silver light like the garden of a dream, the child slept, too, held in the soft clasp of a vision which laid cool fingers of delight on his drowsy lids. When he awoke he lay for a full minute staring into the branches of the olive tree above his head. The gray-green leaves were all alive with a tremulous motion in the fresh morning breeze. A newly-awakened bird trilled softly somewhere in the depths of the garden. The aromatic breath of serried lilies swept his cheek like a caress. It was happiness to have slept—to be once more awake. Then he remembered.

The Roman guards had disappeared—this much Tor perceived at a single glance. A second searching stare told him much more. The door of the tomb gaped wide, beside it stood a young man clad in white garments.

Tor approached this radiant figure unafraid. "Where is the man who opens eyes?" he asked quite simply, for the empty tomb appeared nothing strange to the child newly emerged from his healing dreams.

"He is not here," the young man answered, with grave sweetness. "He is risen, as he said. Behold he goes before you into Galilee; there shall you see him."

Tor opened wide eyes of rapture upon the angel. "My Master is alive!" he whispered to himself. "I shall see him."

He turned as if in a dream, his naked feet making no sound as he brushed, light as the dawn, past the ranks of lilies. There was a woman yonder. She was running from the empty tomb. Tor laughed softly in his joy. "He is alive!" he repeated under his breath.

Chapter 12
Feed My Sheep

To Peter, broken in spirit, bowed down with the shame of his thrice-repeated denials, sleepless with torturing memories of his dead Master, came Mary of Magdalena at dawn of the first day of the week. "They have taken away the Lord out of the tomb," she sobbed, "and I know not where they have laid him."

Peter arose at that word and girded his garments about him that he might run swiftly to the spot. He had no thought of what he should do, but a blind anguish of desire to serve the Master he had scorned drove him forth like a scourge.

He hardly noticed that John, the beloved disciple, was with him, running evenly at his side. Then some murmured word of that other disciple brought a faint memory of words spoken and quickly forgotten, words of painful prophecy, of unearthly hope, which he himself had rejected with scorn and impatience. The Galilean faltered, lagged behind. And so it came to pass that John was first to reach the open tomb.

The rosy light of the new day shone softly into the shadowy sepulcher, revealing the rough-hewn walls, the shallow niche wherein the body had been laid, the folded ceremonial cloths, the scattered spices. The place was fragrant, bright, and mysteriously empty.

Peter stared in at the small, still, empty place, those half-awakened memories stirring strangely within him. "When I have arisen from the dead," he murmured half unconsciously. Had the Master indeed uttered those strange words, or was his brain touched with some sweet madness? He turned to John. The eyes of the beloved disciple were fastened upon the empty niche, his lips moved as in prayer.

With sudden, hard-won resolution Peter entered the tomb, stooping to look more closely at the chill, empty bed with its array of fair linen and odorous spices. He noticed with an awed tightening of the throat that the fine linen cloth which had been wound about the dead man's head was not lying with the other burial garments, but was folded carefully apart, as if the wearer, sitting upon the edge of his couch, had placed it there with a tender thought of the giver.

His bewildered, grief-stricken eyes met the look of dawning hope in the eyes of the other. "He is not here," murmured John, "He is risen!" And suddenly his face became radiant with angelic beauty.

Then the two went away in wondering silence to their own house, and as they went they met other women of their company who told them of angels waiting within the tomb with that question which still sounds in ears grief-sealed against the truth of Omnipresent Life, "Why seek you the living among the dead? Go, tell his disciples and Peter, he goes before you into Galilee, there shall you see him, as he said unto you."

To Galilee, therefore, after certain days of growing hope and marvelous vision, the disciples journeyed in great numbers, and with them went a certain small lad, of a joyous and shining face, no longer a homeless beggar of Jerusalem, but a brother beloved because he had looked upon the King in the beauty of his resurrection body.

It was one of the women, called Salome, who first came upon the child as he walked slowly toward Jerusalem in the dawning day. The little lad was chanting softly to himself the words he had learned on the day of his healing, "Hosanna! Hosanna in the highest! Blessed—blessed is he that comes in the name of the King!"

"Why do you sing, child?" asked the woman. She was still bearing the burden of spices which she had fetched to the empty tomb, and her eyes were red with weeping and anxiety.

"I sing," answered Tor, "because my Master, the King, is alive. He opened my eyes, which were blind as night, and with these eyes have I seen him—alive! Therefore, I sing."

The woman shook her head sorrowfully, for the thing was yet too wonderful for her understanding. "I have seen the empty tomb," she said. "Also I beheld a young man clad in white garments, who declared to us that he was alive, but do not know what to think. How can it be that he is alive when he was dead—

crucified—pierced with a spear?" And again she wept bitterly.

"I saw him," said Tor simply, "the man who opened my eyes. He is alive. I am going to Galilee to see him." And once more the child cried, "Hosanna!" with a clear, jubilant voice.

"Whose child are you, little one?" said the woman, marveling at the brightness of his eyes, which, indeed, shone like the eyes of the angel at the empty tomb. "And where do you live?"

"I have a Father in heaven," said Tor, "and once I had a master who was blind and a beggar, but him I serve no longer, since I serve only the King who gave me my sight."

And when, by questioning the lad, the woman found that he was without kindred and alone in the world, she took him to her own house.

And so it happened that Tor traveled with that great concourse of disciples who went to Galilee to keep the meeting with their risen Lord.

Again Tor met Peter, the Galilean. It was on this wise. The child, enchanted with the beauty of the lake, wandered upon the shore at evening, his eyes wistfully following the fishermen as they put out one after another upon the radiant water. "I should like to sail away in a boat," murmured Tor to himself.

He looked up to find the eyes of Peter fixed upon him. "How came you hither, small one?" asked the fisherman.

"I came from Jerusalem with the woman who is called Salome," answered Tor. "I am come to see my Master, who was dead and is alive again. Already I have seen him. And I shall again see him. Perhaps," he added timidly, "He is there." The child's small finger pointed to the lake, which glowed like a sea of gleaming fire in the dying light.

"Once he came to us walking upon the water," said the fisherman thoughtfully. After a little his eyes wandered to his boats, drawn high and empty upon the shore. There were others of his old comrades nearby, and to these Peter presently called out with something of his old energy, "I will go a fishing," he said.

They answered, "We also will go with you."

And so the boat was made ready, with nets and lanterns, and rough fishermen's gear for possible wild weather in the night watches. Tor watched the preparations with shining eyes. When all was at length finished he bowed himself before Peter after his old beggar's fashion. "I ask earnestly, honorable Galilean, that I also may go fishing," he said timidly.

Peter stared down at him in some perplexity. "What is it that brings you across my path, small one?" he asked, not unkindly. "In Jerusalem you were like my shadow—and now, you will fish."

"I want to see my Master, the King," answered Tor. "He is there." Again the small finger pointed to the darkening lake and the solemn blue mountains beyond. "It is so beautiful he will be there," he repeated softly.

"Come, then," said Peter, and, catching up the little lad, he stowed him snugly in the bow of the great clumsy fishing-craft amid a pile of nets.

Through stretches of moonlit water, where the breeze rippled keenly, in the dark lee of swelling hills, now anchored, now drifting slowly under the winking stars, the fishermen bent to their work. And through the long hours Tor lay quite still in the place where he was bid, speaking to no one, but wrapped in a dream of perfect delight, which the men busied with their fruitless fishing could scarce have understood.

When, now, the darkest hour, that comes before dawn, was already past, and the white mist that shrouded sea and shore and drifted light as thistle-down upon the glassy surface of the nearer water began to glow with rose and amber tints of dawn, Tor wriggled his lithe little body from its nest of coats and stood upright in the bow. His great bright eyes were fixed upon the wavering curtains of the mist. "Listen!" he cried suddenly, in his clear, shrill voice.

A long, level ray from the rising sun burst through the vanishing clouds and rested full upon the land not many furlongs distant.

"Look!" cried the child again, and pointed with his finger.

Someone—a man—was standing upon the pebbly shore looking out over the water. The fishermen rubbed their tired eyes and stared.

"Children, have ye aught to eat!" A clear, human voice brought the little cheerful question across the narrowing space.

"No," shouted the fishermen, satisfied that the friendly voice belonged to some wayfarer, curious as ever to know the luck of an all-night fishing expedition.

"Cast the net on the right side of the boat and ye shall find fish," came the answer.

"Perchance he sees the ripple of a group of fish," muttered Peter, and heaved the great net for another cast.

And now the net sank with its weight of struggling fish. Two of the men leaped hastily into the small boat to secure the catch, but Peter and John were gazing past the heaving net at that solitary figure upon the shore.

"It is the Lord," whispered John. And Peter, with a smothered cry of love and longing, threw his fisherman's coat off and flung himself into the water.

Upon the shore burned a fire of coals, and upon it sputtered a great fish, giving forth appetizing odors to the cool morning air. Beside the fire were piled loaves such as the common people accustomed to eating with this broiled fish. It was all quite common and natural, yet the hands that busied themselves with that simple, satisfying meal bore the mark of the nails.

The fishermen stood with bowed heads, no one daring to ask the question which trembled on every lip.

"Come and break your fast," said their mysterious host, smiling upon their awe-stricken silence. And he took the bread and the fish and gave them to eat.

So when they had eaten, Jesus said to Simon Peter, "Simon, son of John, lovest ye me more than these?"

Peter answered in a half whisper, "Yea, Lord, you knowest that I love you."

Jesus said, "Feed my lambs."

He said to him a second time," Simon, son of John, lovest ye me?"

Again Peter answered with an anguished glance of entreaty, "Yea, Lord; you knowest that I love you."

Again came the command, "Feed my sheep."

He said to him the third time, "Simon, son of John, lovest ye me?"

Then Peter burst into a great passion of weeping, and wept as on the night he had denied his Master. "Lord," he cried out, "you knowest all things. Ye know that I love ye!"

Jesus said, "Feed my sheep." He spoke other words which they never forgot.

Thus did Peter, the Galilean, who was also called Simon, son of John, answer his Master three times by the Sea of Galilee, and then was the bitter memory of his three denials purged from his soul. Verily he loved much, and was therefore forgiven much. And to the end of his days he remembered well both to cherish the lambs committed to his care by the Upper Shepherd, and to tend and feed the sheep both in the fold and in the pasture.

So it was that he no more spoke carelessly or slightingly to the little lad, Tor, but, counting him as a special charge from his risen Lord. He became to him even as a father.

And Tor, growing into manhood, learned many things both strange and beautiful from the world's page, but he found nothing there to blot out the memory of the Man who had opened his eyes. To the end he followed the King, his Master, and Jesus, long since received into the visible heavens over Galilee, yet remained with him, a sweet and satisfying presence.

The End

Other Books from Golden Prairie Press

Two Little Americans in Spanish California by Frances Margaret Fox Before California became a territory of the United States, it was part of Mexico. In 1846 a little American girl and her brother were living at the San Gabriel Mission. Their neighbor was a Spanish girl named Carlota. Will the little American girl become friends with Carlota, even though their political ideas are completely different? Will the little American boy help the U.S. soldiers win the war? Or will the Spanish kill all the Americans? Find out in this delightful book! Originally published in 1908. Recommended for ages 8 to adult.

Jack and Jill by Louisa May Alcott
A tragic accident leaves fun-loving Jill and good-natured Jack cooped up for months. During this time they learn some valuable lessons and are cheered up by their friends. Jill and her two friends begin a missionary society, while Jack helps a troubled youth stay on the straight and narrow. Louisa May Alcott has done an excellent job of showing the real life of children during the 1800s. Originally published in 1880 this timeless tale is just as inspiring and enjoyable today as when it was first written.

www.AmyPuetz.com